Saving Tommy

Ian Gielen

ISBN: 978-1-7640126-0-7

Cover design by Savannah Fischer

Edited by Marked Up Editing

Formatted by Jyl Glenn

Thanks to Julia Lynn Terry for elements of the cover.

Dedicated to my son who is and will always be my world.
I love you with all my heart.

Contents

"You can have no dominion greater or less than that over yourself." — Leonardo da Vinci

Prologue

Tommy

"Hey Tommy boy, where do you think you're going?" Jack yelled out from behind him, a sneer plastered on his face.

Tommy's heart sank as he quickened his pace, eager to get to the sanctuary of the library, but it was too late. Jack and his friends, all from the grade above him, surrounded him, one of them pushing him hard in the back and sending him stumbling.

As soon as he had heard the bell ring signalling the beginning of lunch break, Tommy had rushed to his locker to retrieve his lunchbox, sending furtive glances around him as he did so. Every day since the start of the year, he had been targeted by Jack, a recent addition to the school who had joined his class and who had quickly established himself at the top of the pecking order of school bullies. He had made fast friends with a group of known troublemakers and had begun to target those who they saw as weaker. Tommy had been one of the first to be targeted since he didn't have many friends and preferred to spend his breaks alone in the library between the pages of a book.

Every lunchtime was the same. Jack and his friends would actively seek him out wherever he went, call him names, pinch his belongings, destroy his school books, spit on him, and push him around until one of the teachers on duty eventually took notice. By then, he was so upset that he just wanted to go home, crawl into bed, and leave the world behind.

Something about today though seemed different. The boys had always been cruel, but the sheer anger and hate on their faces today made him tremble in fear. Losing his footing from the force of the push, he fell to the ground, scraping his knee and drawing blood as his lunchbox flew from his grasp, and rested under a nearby bush.

"Look at this loser. Looks like he was heading to the library, like a nerd," Jared, the boy closest to Jack said, stomping on his lunchbox. The lid caved in with a snap of plastic, the juices of the mandarin that had been crushed within leaking out.

The group of boys laughed and cheered, patting Jared on the back as he stood with a proud look on his face.

"Please, just leave me alone," Tommy whispered, his voice barely audible, his eyes welling up with tears.

The group of boys laughed again, making his insides twist as Jack leaned down and grabbed him by the collar of his shirt.

"What did you say? Speak up, loser," he said, shaking him roughly.

Tommy looked around, his vision blurred with tears, trying to see past the faces of his tormentors for someone, anyone, to help. As usual, no one did. The students who walked by either cast sympathetic glances toward him or ignored him completely.

"Hey, how about this time we make him cry for real." Blake, one of the other bullies said, an eager smile on his face as he looked around at the others for approval. His friends pursed their lips and nodded as they began to launch taunts at him, each one more cruel than the last, their words cutting deeper than any physical blow possibly could.

Hot tears streamed down Tommy's face, the bullies' jeering and the sounds of their self-congratulatory slaps a cruel counterpoint to his silent suffering. Tommy raised his hands to his ears, trying to drown out the noise, but one of the boys forced them back down again, screaming into his ear in an attempt to deafen him. Finally, they left him there hunched over on the ground in tears. The band of boys satisfied, yet growing bored from his constant crying.

The words they taunted him with replayed in his mind, seeping into his psyche; each one a dagger that left him reeling with helplessness and loneliness. There was no one who could understand what these words were doing to him, not his friends, his teachers, the counselors, or his mom and dad. He was alone. He considered the times where he had retreated deep within himself to the happy place he sometimes went to when things got too hard. The occasions where he didn't spill tears and didn't react at all were the times when the teasing ended the quickest. Maybe it was time to adopt that method of thought.. If he didn't react, maybe the bullies would eventually leave him alone, if he was consistent enough.

Slowly, he rose to his feet, weakness flooding through his system, his legs trembling in the aftershock of what had happened. He knew this was what he would have to face tomorrow, the day after that, and every other day he was at school. That knowledge and the constant trauma was something he faced daily. The pain, the fear, and the anxiety he felt caused something to shift within him. His thoughts and emotions began to envelop in a fog, numbing the sharp edges of the overwhelming emotions he had felt up to now. His muscles steadied, his fluttering heartbeat returning to normal. He wiped the tears from his eyes, his face now a mask of indifference, a shield to protect what little remained of his fragile heart. He moved mechanically toward the remains of his lunchbox and picked it up. This would be his life now, he vowed. He would no longer let emotions rule his world.

Chapter 1
Boyd

Six months later

"Based on these results, we have a few options," Doctor Selazar said, as he swiveled his chair to face Boyd, Isla, and Tommy.

"Tommy rated with high severity on the Beck Depression Inventory score, which is concerning for his age. I'll give you a script for some antidepressants to start, but we'll need to go further than that to work out what is affecting Tommy here. That will get to the root cause of the problem."

He smiled at Tommy, his eyes crinkling with warmth and reassurance.

Tommy met his gaze with a quick glance of his own before looking back down at his fidget spinner, which he was idly spinning in his lap. His lips pursed in concentration, trying with all his might to quell the panic rising within him as it tried to fight through the thick fog of indifference he had worked so hard on building as the doctor continued speaking.

The Doctor's smile thinned as he turned his focus back on Boyd and Isla.

"Being as young as he is at age ten, there are youth clinics that offer group classes. They focus on building social connections and resilience for those that are facing mental difficulties. Beyond that, there are the tried-and-true child psychology sessions as well. I'd also recommend getting in contact with his school to make sure he's supported through all of this."

"How much money are we looking at, Doc? We are feeling the pinch a bit right now. As you can see, Isla can't work at the moment, and my income barely pays the bills and food as it is."

Boyd's worried expression gave way to one of overwhelming love as he looked at Tommy, his eyes softening.

"I mean, of course we would love to do everything we can for Tommy, but our money can only stretch so far."

With a sympathetic nod, Dr. Selazar's gaze shifted between Isla and Boyd. He sighed as he leant back in his chair, tapping his pen on his desk rhythmically.

"Sadly, you're not alone there. So many people are struggling right now."

He paused, his gaze unfocused as he took a moment to gather his thoughts.

"There is one other option. A free clinical trial for a new treatment that is experimental at this stage."

He leaned closer to Boyd and Isla, his gaze serious and unwavering, a hardened look on his face.

"Keep in mind though, as this is experimental, effects may vary and can be unpredictable."

"At this point, we will try anything as long as it doesn't cost an arm and a leg," Isla said, hope filling her voice.

Doctor Selazar leant back in his chair, turning his attention back to Tommy, who was doing his best to pretend he wasn't there, before he sighed again and swivelled his chair back toward the computer.

"Let me just pull up the information."

He tapped a few keys on the keyboard, and the printer whirred to life.

Boyd and Isla exchanged hopeful glances before they both looked at Tommy, their brows furrowed in concern.

"Here you go," Doctor Selazar said as he handed Boyd a flyer.

At the top of the flyer was a prominent, minimalist logo: a brain shape enclosing the letters "NB," with "NeuroBalance Institute" printed beneath. Boyd and Isla shuffled closer together as they scanned the document, their eyes widening at the same exact moment before they looked up at Doctor Selazar incredulously.

"This can't be real, surely," Boyd said, placing the flyer on his lap.

"Oh, it's very real. The NeuroBalance Institute hasn't been around for long, but they have shown promise. This information has only come out to doctors in the last few days, so it's very new. As such, and given the severity of his depression, there is a good chance that Tommy here can partake in this, if that is your decision, of course."

A flicker of uncertainty danced in Boyd's eyes as they darted from the flyer on his lap to Isla's worried frown, the Doctor's steady gaze, and Tommy's nervous, yet unreadable countenance.

"How about we ask Tommy if he's interested?" Doctor Selazar prompted Isla and Boyd, who were both still dumbstruck at what they'd read.

Boyd nodded mutely before handing the flyer back to the Doctor.

"Tommy, would you be interested in your very own wellness pet? It would help and guide you through this difficult period you're going through. Not only that, but it would be bonded to you and could become as close as a family member. Would you like that?"

Tommy continued to play with the fidget spinner, ignoring the doctor completely.

"Here, take a look at this. It might help you visualise what I'm talking about."

Doctor Selazar slid the flyer onto Tommy's lap, positioning it underneath the fidget spinner so that his eyes would fall on it.

The flyer detailed a genetically engineered creature called the Bliss Buddy that was specifically designed to support those with mental illnesses between the ages of six to twelve. Because of its enhanced intelligence and acute senses, it could perceive its owner's needs and adjust its behavior to provide the best possible assistance. One of the creatures was depicted at the center of the flyer. Its wide, sympathetic, intelligent eyes were set into a face that invoked instant comfort. This particular creature had the sleek fur and pointed ears of a cat but stood on two legs.

Tommy's toy spun slower and slower, his eyes diverting and fixing on the flyer before his eyes widened, a flicker of something akin to excitement crossing his face. A smile formed tentatively on his lips and in his eyes. Shining with cautious excitement, they met Boyd's and Isla's loving gaze.

Boyd and Isla exchanged a shocked, meaningful glance, their smiles mirroring one another. It had been so long since they'd seen Tommy show any emotion, let alone get excited about something. Boyd knew as soon as they saw his reaction that the decision was made for them. He would do anything to keep that smile on Tommy's face, and he knew Isla felt the same. If this was what it took, they would do it.

"Well, I guess there's your answer Doc," Boyd laughed, Isla joining in as Tommy's expression lightened further with excitement.

"Excellent," Doctor Selazar said, looking on with a broad smile.

"I'll just send in Tommy's results to them. They will match one of their pets to his needs and get in contact with you."

Tommy began to bounce on his chair, still silent, but his excitement was almost palpable.

"Thank you so much, Doc," Boyd whispered, his eyes shining with unshed tears as he took Isla's hand and gave it a squeeze.

Beaming from ear to ear, Boyd and Isla's smiles remained fixed as they drove home. Boyd couldn't help but sneak looks in the rearview mirror as an excited looking Tommy emitted small sporadic smiles of his own while he gazed out the window at the passing scenery. Boyd's heart swelled with hope for the first time in months. He glanced at Isla, seeing her face alight with a similar burgeoning hope. Could this strange, almost mythical pet that sounded like a fairytale actually hold the key to bringing their son back to them?

Chapter 2

Isla

O*ne week later*

Isla slotted the last plate into the dishwasher, closing it to the accompanying sound of the rattle of dishes. With effort, she rose from her wheelchair, her feet unsteady as she leaned over the kitchen bench to wash her hands, just as the doorbell rang.

She grabbed a hand-towel and dried her hands, tossing it haphazardly back next to the kitchen sink before gingerly lowering herself back into the wheelchair, and making her way to the door.

She opened it to a woman wearing a plastic smile that screamed corporate. Her outfit of slacks, fitted business shirt, and jacket completed the picture. Two men, dressed in crisp navy-blue suits, stood just behind her, the same plastic smile on their faces.

"Can I help you?" She asked with a frown, as she studied the trio.

"If you're here to sell something…"

"Oh no, of course not," the lady before her chuckled, as she extended her hand.

"My name is Janet. I'm the head of Customer Relations at the NeuroBalance Institute. This is Andre and Jack, both research assistants. I assume you're Isla?"

"Ahh yes, that's right," Isla said, a relieved smile replacing her confused frown as she grasped Janet's hand in a firm handshake.

"I hear your son is having a few difficulties navigating life at the moment. I think we have the perfect solution for him." Her forced smile softened into a warm, genuine one that lit up her eyes.

"God, I hope so," Isla breathed, her hopeful yet anxious tone earning a sympathetic nod from the three.

"Please come in."

She wheeled back to make way for Janet. Before she entered, she turned and signalled to the two men who nodded and returned to the van parked outside in the driveway, the large NeuroBalance Institute logo plastered on its side.

Janet turned back to smile at Isla as she strode past into the living room, stopping to take in her surroundings.

"A lovely house you've got here," she said, nodding with approval.

"Thank you, we only just moved in six months ago."

With a nod, Janet's eyes turned inquisitively to the wheelchair.

"I hope you don't mind me asking, but how did you come to be in a wheelchair? Sorry to be so blunt, but we just need to make sure we have all the information about our new pet owners."

Noticing the wary expression on Isla's face, she quickly followed up, "You know, just for insurance purposes."

Isla's eyes flickered with comprehension. "Oh, of course," she said.

"I dislocated my hip at work a couple of weeks ago."

"That sounds painful, to say the least," Janet said, wincing sympathetically.

"Oh, it definitely was," Isla said with a grimace. "The perils of getting older and being a Pilates instructor. Would not recommend," she said, rubbing her hip instinctively.

Janet laughed, turning her attention to the two men entering through the door, one with a small animal carrier in hand, the other with a cardboard box overflowing with supplies.

"Ok, here he is. Now he's a bit shy and it might take a few days before he comes out of his shell, but he will. He's a ninety-five percent match for Tommy and his needs, which is one of the highest percentile matches we've had so far."

"How many of these, ah, pets are in homes now?" Isla asked with a nervous hitch in her voice.

"We are lucky enough to have twenty families involved in our program now, with many more to come," Janet said, noting the hesitation in Isla's voice.

"Now, before we let him out, is Tommy here by any chance? We can't leave our pet here without seeing how he and the child respond to each other, just for safety reasons, of course."

Isla recoiled, visibly startled.

"Safety reasons?"

"Oh sorry, I didn't mean to alarm you. It's just that we need to be assured that your child has the ability to interact with and handle our pet."

"Oh, of course," Isla said with a nervous smile.

"Tommy, your new pet has arrived. Do you want to meet him?" she called out toward the stairs.

Above them, the quick patter of eager feet in response heralded Tommy's approach, causing all four to smile.

"He's been upstairs decorating for Halloween. It's his favourite season," Isla smiled affectionately as Tommy ran downstairs, skipping steps in his haste to reach them.

"Careful, careful," Isla said with a laugh.

Tommy jumped off the last few steps and hastened toward the cage, his face lit up with excitement.

"Well, it looks like someone is excited," Janet laughed, her eyes twinkling in amusement.

"Alright then, let's not waste any time."

She positioned the cage so the entrance faced Tommy and lifted the latch on the small door, pulling it open with care to let the creature out.

Everyone collectively held their breath as a paw slid out cautiously to grip the side of the cage before the small furry figure emerged nervously, facing Tommy.

Isla gasped in shock at the sight of it, her face paling. The creature was about twenty inches tall, the majority of its body covered in cloudlike soft ginger-white fur. Trembling with fear, it tentatively took small steps forward.

Standing on two legs that ended in paws, it had the body of a small squat cat complete with tail. The center of its chest was hairless, revealing black leathery skin. Its head had the angular sharp look of a bat, hairless apart from the fur lining its forehead between its long and pointed leathery ears. Its large intelligent cat-like eyes were filled with uncertainty as it gazed at its surroundings. A series of hesitant, almost inaudible squeaks escaped it, its eyes flitting nervously before locking onto Tommy's welcoming smile.

With hesitant, hopeful eyes, it extended its arms toward Tommy, its face softening with a small gentle smile as it took slow, careful steps forward.

"It's so... It's so strange..." Isla whispered, looking upon the creature in awe.

"How is it possible that I can know what it's feeling just by looking at it?"

"That's exactly how we designed it. We wanted it to be obvious for anyone so that people can know what it, as well as its owner, might be feeling." Janet said proudly, a smile playing on her lips as she crossed her arms over her chest, watching the interaction between Tommy and the creature.

Cooing softly, the creature came within arm's length of Tommy, who was staring at it in awe, the softness in his face already reflecting his affection for the creature. The two came together and embraced, the small creature's arms barely extending to Tommy's elbow.

The sight warmed Isla's heart. She had been so used to seeing Tommy's expressionless face over the last six months that seeing any emotion, especially excitement and the few early signs of happiness, filled her with hope.

No matter what she and Boyd had tried, whether it be trying to coax out his feelings, spending quality time together at parks and social events, even just being there for him—none of it had any impact on Tommy's condition. Maybe this could be the start of something. Maybe after all the heartache, she and Boyd would have their boy back again, as happy and carefree as he once was, given time.

After watching them interact for a few minutes, Janet motioned to Isla, indicating she wanted to speak to her in private. Reaching into the box of supplies, Janet retrieved a folder and headed toward the kitchen. With a last look toward Tommy, Isla pivoted the wheelchair to follow Janet, stopping at the doorway to the kitchen where she could keep an eye on him.

"It seems as though they have taken quite a shine to each other," Janet stated, with a broad smile on her face.

"I just wanted to go over a few details before I leave you both to it."

She handed over the folder.

"Inside, you will find detailed instructions on care, including bedding, food, what to do in case of an injury and a schedule of our visitations to see how everything is going."

She paused for a moment, a flicker of something unidentifiable coming over her eyes.

"There is also a safe word in case something goes wrong with the creature."

Janet stiffened at the words, casting a worried glance toward the creature.

"Not that anything will, of course," Janet said quickly, noticing her body language.

"It's just in case of an emergency. We have incorporated a safe word that will render the creature immobile. A factory reset if you will. The word is 'Fermare' which is Italian for stop. We had to come up with a word not normally used in everyday language and well, our founder is Italian, so we thought it would be appropriate." She gave Isla a reassuring smile.

"Other than that, we are pretty much set." She stopped to dig around in her jacket, producing a card with her contact details.

"Here is our number if you need anything at all. Call anytime, day or night, ok?"

Isla nodded numbly, her mind absorbing what Janet had said about the safe word. If they had to incorporate that, did it mean that there could be some potential danger to her son?

She was just about to voice her concerns when the front door opened and Boyd walked in. Amidst the flurry of introductions, Boyd's shocked reaction at seeing the creature and watching it and Tommy together, her concerns were soon forgotten. The events after that were a blur, and before they knew it, Janet, Andre and Jack had left, and Boyd and Isla were on the couch watching Tommy and his new pet playing on the floor in the lounge room.

"It's remarkable, isn't it?" Boyd said, watching Tommy roll a small bouncy plastic ball toward his pet, its paws deftly stopping and rolling it back, a bizarre, almost human-like smile playing on the pet's leathery face. Somehow, that smile looked completely natural.

"Its name isn't 'It' daddy," Tommy said, his eyes locked onto his pet. "It's Bobby," he said proudly, his face radiating happiness.

Isla and Boyd exchanged shocked looks before giving each other huge smiles. This was the first time he'd spoken in months. So many tears of heartache, frustration and sadness had been shed when they had tried everything they could think of just to get him to show some semblance of interest in life. Now here he was, smiling and talking.

Isla's injury had meant that her job and Pilates business had been put on hold and put a strain on their finances, so they hadn't been able to afford therapy or seek any other means of assistance that required money. Tears of pure unadulterated happiness fell from their eyes as they clasped each other's hands, watching Tommy and his pet play. If the presence of this strange creature was what it took to begin the process of getting their boy back, then they would do anything to make it work.

The night passed quickly. Too quickly for Boyd and Isla, who lost themselves in the throes of enjoyment watching their boy with Bobby. It was almost nine o'clock before Isla became aware of the time. After reading the bedtime instructions in the information booklet she retrieved from the dining room table, she asked Boyd to prepare a makeshift bed for Bobby on the floor next to Tommy's bed, using blankets from the linen closet. With a firm grip on Bobby's hand, Tommy followed Boyd's lead, their footsteps echoing on the wooden stairs. By the time she managed to wheel herself to the stairs, pick up her walking stick, go up, and switch to another waiting wheelchair at the top, Tommy had already started his bedtime routine. Smiling, she watched Tommy lead Bobby around, hand in paw, chatting and explaining everything he did.

Isla left them to it, and after completing her bedtime routine, she limped her way with the walking stick into Tommy's room, where he lay in bed, gazing in adoration at Bobby, who was tucked under the blankets on his own little makeshift bed. Bobby was returning his gaze with a heartfelt smile, his affection for the boy apparent.

She couldn't help but smile at the heartwarming sight. With each passing month, Tommy's unchanging state had pushed her closer to despair. The powerlessness she felt was like a physical weight on her chest, and she had felt the cold grip of depression tightening around her like a noose. No matter who she had talked to about the situation, she had felt like a failure, a heavy cloak of inadequacy that no conversation seemed to lift. Now, after months of heartache, Tommy was talking, smiling, and playing. His eyes sparkling with newfound life, completely changed in just a few scant hours with Bobby. She could only hope that Tommy's newfound enthusiasm for life, so vibrant and evident on his first day with Bobby, would endure beyond the initial thrill of his arrival.

Tommy tore his gaze away from Bobby, a shy smile of pure happiness lighting up his face as he looked at her; Bobby, following his gaze, mirrored his smile. The sight of the pet's smile toward her froze her own for a moment. The unnatural sight of the strange creature mimicking her son's behavior was unsettling. She shook it off. She would no doubt get used to it after a while. She smiled back at Bobby, limping with difficulty over to place a kiss on Tommy's forehead, and retreated back towards the door.

"Wait, you didn't give Bobby a kiss. You have to give Bobby a kiss. It's the rules."

"Oh, it's the rules, is it?"

Isla laughed at the overly serious expression on Tommy's face.

"Oh, well, we can't break the rules now, can we?" she said gravely, her expression changing to one of mock seriousness.

She stepped forward and bent down, gingerly brushing her lips over the cool leathery skin on Bobby. Suppressing a shudder, she straightened and gave a grave nod toward Tommy.

"That's better," Tommy said, a smile on his face as he looked down at Bobby to gauge his reaction. Bobby grinned, his eyes shining with mischief in response.

Isla laughed and headed back toward the doorway, taking one last look at the pair.

"Goodnight boys. Don't let the bedbugs bite," she said, with a mischievous smile.

She had just started to walk away when she heard a tinny high-pitched voice say, "bedbug". She froze in her tracks.

"Bedbug," the voice repeated, "Bedbug, bedbug, bedbug, bedbug."

"No way," she breathed, turning around and peering in through the doorway.

Tommy was sitting upright in his bed, his wide, amazed eyes fixed on Bobby, whose paws clapped excitedly, a soft patting sound filling the room.

"Bedbug," Bobby said again, his tiny mouth working hard to shape the human words it wasn't designed to speak.

"Mommy, are you seeing this? He's saying bedbug!" A peal of laughter erupted from Tommy, causing Bobby to respond with a flurry of excited, high-pitched yips, a miniature, frantic echo of Tommy's delight.

The whole sight was charming yet unnerving. She was certain the pet wasn't supposed to be able to speak, and Janet definitely had not mentioned it. She would have to double check the information booklet again and send a message to Janet in any case. If it could learn to speak, what else would it be eventually able to do?

"Ok boys, now it's really time for bed," she said after a few moments, clapping her hands to get their attention.

Both Tommy and Bobby slumped down under the covers, looking chagrined but sneaking sly smiles at each other.

"Goodnight," she said with a smile of her own before flipping off the light and closing the door gently behind her.

Just as she was about to leave, the sound of a tiny, muffled voice hissing "Bedbug" was followed by a hushed giggle from behind the door.

The sound of the whisper sent a chill down Isla's spine. The entire exchange just felt wrong. Unnatural. Bobby was a creature that should not be-but was, and he had already seemingly evolved outside the boundaries of what he was created to do.

With care, she made her way back down the stairs, forgoing the wheelchair much to her hip's protest. Ignoring it and knowing she would pay for it tomorrow, she retrieved the information about the creature from the box downstairs and scanned it. As she had thought, there was no mention of the creature ever being able to talk. Dumping the information back in the box, she hurried back upstairs as fast as she could, finally limping into the master bedroom and heading straight for her phone on her nightstand. She sent off a text to Janet before even acknowledging Boyd, who was sitting bare chested in the bed, book in hand, looking at her in confusion.

"Everything ok?" he asked, his brows furrowed with concern when he saw the worry etched on her face.

She set the phone down, sighed, and settled onto the mattress, hoisting her legs up with a groan and then inching herself back until her shoulders rested against the headboard.

"I think we may have made a mistake accepting this... thing... this... pet into our lives," she said, wringing her hands to accentuate her point.

"Why? What's happened?" With a concerned look, Boyd straightened, setting the book aside to look at her.

"It talked Boyd, the damn thing talked!" she said, her voice rising. As soon as she noticed how loud she was being, she looked toward the doorway nervously.

"You're kidding," he said, his eyes widening in disbelief.

"I wish I was," she muttered.

"I just sent a message to Janet, asking if it's normal. I'm pretty sure it's not. The information they left didn't mention it and neither did she when she was here. Boyd, if this thing can talk, imagine what else it could do that's not in the information booklet. I don't trust it and I'm starting to think it's not safe."

Boyd hesitated, chewing his lip thoughtfully, before nodding slowly.

"How about we get Janet to come and check it out tomorrow? You can see how much Tommy loves it; he would be devastated if we took Bobby away. He's only just come out of his shell. Who knows what effect it would have on him?"

Isla sighed, her forehead creased with worry.

Just then, a frantic vibration from her phone startled her. Reaching for it, she saw it was a text from Janet. Unlocking her phone with a swipe, she read the message, let out another sigh, and returned it to her nightstand.

"She says it's unusual but nothing to worry about. She will come to check it out on Thursday."

"Okay, well, that's only two days away. I guess we'll just need to keep a close eye on things until then, yeah? Will you be ok with that?"

"I guess I don't really have a choice," she said, biting at her nails absently.

"Come here," Boyd said, lying down with outstretched arms.

She reluctantly shifted herself closer, fell into his embrace, and instantly felt calmer. There was something about hearing his strong heartbeat that never failed to calm her down. Despite her worry, tonight was no exception.

"I just want Tommy to be happy, Boyd. Seeing his smile, hearing his laughter today, it was everything. I can't help but think I've been a terrible mother to him. If I wasn't, he wouldn't need this pet. I tried so hard but just couldn't get through to him, to give him what he needs."

Tears poured down her cheeks, each sob a tremor in her body as she tried to stifle her grief, fearing Tommy would hear.

"Baby, you did everything you could and more. I couldn't reach him either. There's nothing more either of us could have done."

His tears, warm and heavy, fell onto her as he rocked her, each drop a silent testament to his own grief.

"Let's try to make this work, yeah? Hopefully, talking is just the extent of what it can do."

Isla opened her mouth to reluctantly agree when, just then, the pitter patter of paws could be heard retreating from just outside the bedroom door, heading down the hall toward Tommy's bedroom.

Chapter 3

Boyd

"What the fuck?" Boyd exclaimed, springing from bed and running into the hallway. The dim lighting from the bedside lamp that spilled out from the bedroom didn't provide enough light to see down its entire length, but he thought he could see slight movement at the door to Tommy's bedroom.

He crept down the hallway, trying to remain as quiet as possible until he reached the door. He frowned, noticing that the door was slightly ajar. Tommy always liked to sleep with the door closed. He sometimes left the door open in his rush to return to bed from the bathroom in the dead of night, but he and Isla had not heard the toilet flushing this time.

He pushed the bedroom door open. Darkness greeted him, the only light a weak spill from the hallway light opposite that did little to illuminate the small, makeshift bed near Tommy's as he searched for the creature. There it was, fast asleep, its small body barely visible under the thick, woven blanket which rose and fell with each quiet breath. He shifted his gaze to Tommy and saw him tucked under his covers as usual, breathing deeply and sound asleep.

He moved his gaze back to the creature, frowning as he studied it. Though it gave no indication of being awake, if it had the ability to observe them, mimicking sleep would be a simple task for it. Could it be possible it understood what they were saying? If so, that opened up a whole new avenue of problems. There was no doubt now that both he and Isla would have to keep a close eye on things from here on.

He closed the door and headed back toward the bedroom.

"The damn thing was in its bed, looking for all the world to be asleep, but I know we didn't imagine it, that little freak must've been spying on us," he hissed at Isla, who was sitting propped up in the bed.

Astonished and speechless, she opened her mouth as if to speak, but then closed it again, the shock rendering her unable to utter a single word. Silently, he drew her to him and held her tightly, both sharing the same sense of foreboding. It was a long time before either of them felt comfortable enough to switch the light off and drift away into a restless night's sleep.

Chapter 4

Isla

Isla wheeled herself to the top of the stairs and grabbed her walking stick from the attached holder, using it to brace herself and stand. Each step to the bottom was taken with caution, the muffled sound of Tommy's giggle drifting from the lounge room a comforting sound. Despite the exhaustion she felt after barely sleeping last night and her worries about the new pet, hearing the unabashed, innocent joy in her son's voice brought a smile to her face. Settling herself into the wheelchair near the stairs, she wheeled herself to the lounge room, peering in to watch Tommy and Bobby from the entrance.

Picking up their ball game from the previous night, Tommy was mixing up his throws and rolls, changing his pace between each to see how Bobby would react.

As she watched, Tommy giggled, his arm coiling back like a spring before he hurled the small rubber ball with all his might toward Bobby. Isla winced, expecting a thud of impact, but the creature's quick reflexes were amazing; it caught the ball, its arm yielding slightly to cushion the blow.

The creature's smile was unsettling, a wide, unnatural stretch of its jaw that revealed rows of needle-sharp teeth, before it tossed the ball back with care.

"Tommy, be careful with Bobby, okay? We don't want to hurt him, do we?"

"It's ok mommy, really. He catches everything. He's amazing!"

She sat there and watched as the game continued, cringing on occasion when she was sure Bobby would be hit by a particularly hard and difficult to catch throw, but he never was. The little creature showed amazing reflexes, no matter how quickly Tommy threw the ball, catching it and returning it to Tommy with surprising gentleness.

A small smile playing on her lips, Isla rolled toward the kitchen.

"Have you boys had breakfast yet?" She called out.

"Not yet mommy, we've been too busy,"

"Okay, I'll get it ready for you," she called back.

She hummed a tune as she placed a cup under the coffee maker and pressed the button for a double shot cappuccino. Next, she poured Cocoa Krispies into two bowls and got the milk from the fridge. Ordinarily, Tommy would do this himself, but she was just so overjoyed that he was back to talking and laughing that she didn't mind. After retrieving the coffee and pouring in some creamer, she wheeled back to the kitchen table.

"Alright, breakfast is ready," she called out, taking a sip from her warm cup, already anticipating she would need more than her usual dose of caffeine to get through the day. Neither she nor Boyd had slept well, both of them tossing and turning, their worries about the events of the day and their new pet a heavy weight on their chests.

"Come on, I'll race you!" Tommy shouted, his voice echoing from the lounge room, the playful challenge followed by the patter of small bare feet slapping against the tiles.

Tommy rounded the corner with a skid, looking back over his shoulder and squealing in excitement when he saw the small creature not far behind, its little legs pumping and a look of determination on its face as it followed.

Stumbling to adjust his footing as he changed direction, Tommy was off balance when the small furry form of Bobby launched itself at him, landing on his chest, a tuft of his shirt clenched in its sharp claws. Tommy collapsed to the floor on his back with the small creature still attached, laughing uproariously. Bobby settled onto Tommy's chest, its head cocked inquisitively, large eyes studying him intently before it let out a series of soft, gurgling sounds in an attempt to copy Tommy's laughter. The sight of his pet's awkward mimicry sent Tommy into a fit of laughter, tears rolling down his cheeks.

Isla watched on with mixed emotions, equal parts happy that her son had found his joy again and unnerved at the once again unnatural behaviour of the creature. While grateful for the happiness it brought Tommy, an unshakeable feeling of distrust towards the creature persisted. Its mimicking behaviour looked innocent enough to the naked eye, yet a subtle wrongness permeated its movements; every action felt cold and premeditated, each response too precise, too devoid of genuine emotion.

Rising to his feet, Tommy held the creature close to his chest.

"Honey, oh no, your shirt," Isla said, staring at Tommy's chest. A small, ragged hole had been torn in its center, revealing a scratch beneath from Bobby's sharp claws. Blood welled up from the scratch, staining the torn edges of his shirt.

"Oh honey, are you ok?" Isla asked, her brows knitted in concern as she wheeled herself over to him.

Tommy calmly placed the creature on one of the chairs at the kitchen table before straightening to examine himself.

"Oh, umm yeah, I think so. It doesn't hurt at all," he said, a small smile still plastered on his face.

"Let me get it fixed up for you."

As she wheeled toward the first-aid cabinet, she glanced back toward Tommy in concern but was instead drawn toward the strange look on Bobby's face, a look that sent a chill down her spine.

Chapter 5

Isla

Bobby was seated on the kitchen chair that Tommy had placed him in, his eyes set on the bloody wound on Tommy's chest. His small body was rigid, his wide unblinking eyes reflecting the dim light that seeped in from the small kitchen window, a disturbing smile stretched across his lips as his wet, leathery nose twitched as if in agitation.

She continued to watch it as she gathered the antiseptic, wipes, and band-aid, and made her way over to Tommy. All the while, the creature sat there unmoving, only the rise and fall of its chest betraying its otherwise toylike appearance.

Using a cloth to clean the wound first, she gently dabbed it around the angry-looking skin to the accompanying wince of Tommy. Seeing his reaction, Bobby jolted out of his trance and whipped his head toward Isla, his teeth bared in a snarl, a low growl vibrating in his chest, making the hairs on Isla's arms stand on end. Her eyes widened as she flinched, lifting her hands to show she meant no harm.

"It's ok Bobby, I'm not trying to hurt him. I need to clean his wound before I can treat it, and it's going to cause some discomfort."

The creature hesitated, its eyes burning with distrust, its gaze flickering between her and Tommy. When it saw Tommy nod in agreement with her, it relaxed a little, its sharp, bared teeth retreating behind lips that softened and closed.

With caution, she resumed cleaning, with Bobby watching her every movement closely. When it came time to apply the antiseptic, she paused once more.

"Now I have to apply the antiseptic. Tommy might cry out a bit in pain because it will sting, but it's needed to remove any bacteria that might infect the wound. OK?"

Bobby didn't respond. Instead, he stared in concern at Tommy as she applied the antiseptic to a cotton bud. Taking a deep breath, she began to dab at the wound. Even with her gentle touch, the antiseptic's sharp sting made Tommy yelp. Bobby instantly lunged, teeth bared in a snarl, his face contorted with protective rage, stopping a hair's breadth from her hand, the gnashing of his teeth a clear warning.

"Bobby, no, stop it," Tommy said, his face draining of color, his lips trembling slightly.

"Mommy is just trying to help me."

Tommy's eyes were wide with a desperate fear, and Bobby, shrinking back in his chair, lowered his gaze, shame evident in his posture.

"Now behave and let mommy help, ok?"

The creature nodded slowly, its eyes downcast. Keeping a wary eye on the creature, Isla continued treating the wound until the band-aid was finally put in place. The creature didn't stir from its position until Isla finished, its eyes blinking slowly as it looked up at Tommy, its brow furrowing in what looked like thought.

As if Isla wasn't on edge enough, just seeing it reacting this way was almost enough for her to call the NeuroBalance Institute and have them collect it right now, but she resisted. Despite the aggression it had shown, it had stopped short of an attack, its reactions clearly based on its desire to protect Tommy. She could feel an icy pit of panic forming in her stomach. She needed to talk to Janet before the creature's bond with Tommy became too strong; otherwise, removing it if it came to that might send Tommy back to square one, or even worse.

"There you go, good as new," she said, forcing a smile as she kissed his forehead.

"Now off you go. Go on and change your shirt and come back down for breakfast. You'll need all the energy you can get for the big day ahead with Bobby here, no doubt," she smiled and indicated to Bobby, who was still intently watching Tommy.

"OK mom," Tommy said with a big smile. He shifted his attention to Bobby.

"Just wait here for me, OK? I'll be right back."

Bobby nodded in response, his eyes still unnervingly wide as they tracked Tommy's progress up the stairs and out of view.

Chapter 6

Isla

With an inward sigh, Isla wheeled back to the medicine cabinet and replaced the supplies. She paused there and rubbed her throbbing head, feeling the beginnings of a stress headache. Grabbing the aspirin, she popped a few and downed them without water. The day had only just begun, and she was already struggling. She dreaded thinking about what else might happen over the course of the day.

Wheeling herself back to the kitchen table, she took a sip of her now lukewarm coffee, setting the mug down, her eyes meeting Bobby's steady gaze. His eyes, though back to their normal size, held a strange, unsettlingly analytic glint. A palpable sense of disapproval hung in the air, as if he was assessing her and finding her wanting. Isla shivered despite herself, feeling icy tingles shoot down her spine. The creature's intense stare felt charged with growing animosity; a tangible dislike that intensified with every second of his unwavering focus. His long leathery ears began to twitch as if in agitation. Beads of sweat started to form on Isla's forehead, and she admonished herself when she noticed. This was ridiculous. She was reading too much into things. She must be. It was more than likely that the events of last night and this morning had caused her to be overly cautious around the creature, and the lack of sleep wasn't helping. It would all be sorted out when

Janet came to visit, she was sure, but for now she'd pretend to be happy Bobby was there, hiding her true feelings of unease.

She returned Bobby's persistent stare with a smile. The creature froze. His ears stopped their twitching, as a frown etched itself onto his leathery forehead, his eyes blinking in confusion.

"I hope you're having a good time with Tommy. He absolutely loves you, you know?"

Bobby gazed at her quietly, tilting his head as if trying to understand why she had switched from looking uneasy to acting more welcoming all of a sudden.

"Just try to be careful with him, OK? He's been through a lot and though he's come out of his shell for you, we need to treat him gently and with care. Do you think you can do that?"

Isla didn't expect an answer or for him to understand in the slightest, so she was shocked to see the creature nod, his features softening slightly as he took in her words.

A flurry of footsteps from the direction of the stairs drew both their attention to the entrance to the kitchen. Tommy burst through, skidding to a stop at the kitchen table wearing a shirt that was one size too small, with a faded logo of one of his favorite cartoons. Isla sighed, a small smile playing on her lips as she shook her head, a mixture of amusement and exasperation in her expression.

"You know you have shirts that actually fit you, you know?" She said with a short, amused chuckle.

"I know, but I love this tone. It might be the last time I get to wear it."

His words made her pause. He was right. She had been so consumed this whole year with worry about him that she hadn't realised how much he'd grown right before her eyes. Memories of him in that shirt, when it still fit him, flooded her thoughts like a slideshow. Here was

Tommy, lounging on the couch with a big smile on his face, watching the very show that was depicted by the logo on his shirt. He was giggling and laughing to himself as Isla and Boyd rushed through their morning routine. Here was Tommy chatting excitedly to her about what had happened in the latest episode as Isla prepared her plan for her upcoming Pilates class, absentmindedly nodding but not taking in what he said. Here was Tommy, pointing out the toys from the show as they walked by a shop, Isla too busy texting her friend to organise a night out to notice the disappointment in his eyes. Scene after scene played in her head, bringing tears to her eyes. Consumed by work and their daily routines, she and Boyd hadn't realized how quickly time was slipping away, stealing precious moments with Tommy that they would never get back. Tommy had deserved so much more than they had given him. It was no wonder that he didn't confide in them about his worries and problems when they didn't even make enough time to be present for him when he had none.

"Mommy, are you crying?" Tommy asked, the look of concern on his small face making her tear up even more. Taking a deep breath, she got a tissue from the box on the table and dabbed at her eyes.

"No, I've just got dry eyes is all," she said, with a reassuring smile.

"Now go on, eat your breakfast."

"What about Bobby?" He said, looking at Bobby and seeing he had nothing on the table in front of him.

"Oh, of course, sorry, I completely forgot. I'll go and get his right now."

She maneuvered her wheelchair to the box of supplies Janet's crew had left behind, and from a smaller box within, labeled 'Breakfast', she retrieved a packet.

She held it up before her to study it. It was in a silver packet with a tearaway top. She scanned the feeding directions and saw that it contained a form of reconstituted meat and that it should be stored in the fridge. She cringed, knowing that it should have been put away yesterday. Picking out the rest of the food boxes and placing them in her lap, she made her way to the fridge and put them in, arranging them neatly on the bottom shelf before retrieving a plate from the cupboard and returning to the kitchen table.

Tommy held off eating his cereal, waiting for Bobby to receive his food. A smile spread across Isla's face. Tommy had always been a polite boy. They didn't have to even mention any table manners or etiquette, he had learned them just by observing. In many ways, he had always been self-sufficient. Perhaps that was another reason why they hadn't noticed his gradual downward spiral. She inwardly berated herself again. There was no excuse for letting him slip into the darkness he had been in before Bobby's arrival. She and Boyd had a lot to answer for and she knew they had to change if they were to keep Tommy in a happy place.

She tore the silver packet open and squeezed out the mushy, meaty substance onto the plate in front of Bobby, unsure of how it would eat without cutlery. With a happy bounce in its seat, the small creature watched, its nose twitching as it eyed the meat oozing onto its plate. Tommy laughed at him before starting his cereal, his eyes glimmering with anticipation and excitement for the day ahead.

Moving back to her spot at the table, she gazed with curiosity at the creature as it lifted the plate in its paws and began to lap up the meat. Its long, slender tongue was reminiscent of a snake with a fork at the end. It scooped the mush onto its tongue before it rolled up and retracted back into its mouth, swallowing it without chewing.

It really was an amazing creature despite how uncomfortable it made her feel. Her admiration for it grew the more she thought about it and what its presence meant. Not only had it pulled Tommy out of his shell, but it had also made her realise, with a pang of guilt, what she had missed in Bobby's life, and the mistakes she and Boyd had made in raising him. Sometimes the most obvious things weren't so obvious, until something in life changes your perspective and you can suddenly see with clarity. It felt like a gift and a punishment at the same time, a bittersweet experience. Once again, tears welled in her eyes, blurring her vision as she thought of all the lost moments she and Boyd had missed with Tommy, a wave of grief washing over her. Each tear shed fuelled her resolve; she would use this pain, this bitter knowledge, to become a better mother.

The sound of clattering cutlery announced Tommy and Bobby finishing up their breakfast as they abandoned their seats at the kitchen table in favor of the lounge room. With a tired smile, Isla cleared the table and loaded the dirty dishes into the dishwasher before following them. Again, she sat there, speechless with surprise, as she watched them. Tommy had pulled out the Uno cards and had begun to play Bobby as if he was just another player. Bobby was holding the cards in his paw, his claws extended to hold them in place and was studying them and the card on the top of the discard pile. As she watched, he placed the red seven on top of the red four in the discard pile and waited for Bobby's turn. Tommy wore a big smile on his face as the two took turns until he eventually emerged as the winner.

With each activity the duo did together, Isla felt a growing sense of wonder, her eyes wide with amazement at every turn. From the strategic moves of chess to the artistic flow of drawing, and even the passive absorption of television, Bobby learned at a pace that defied belief. As Isla watched on, she could feel her anxiety rise, a tight knot forming in her stomach. The creature's ability to learn, participate, and emulate Tommy's behavior was effortless; a disturbing mimicry that felt eerily unnatural and too perfect.

As midday approached, Tommy and Bobby were lounging on the couch watching TV, when a drone advertisement flashed across the screen. Tommy sat bolt upright, his eyes wide with excitement, a grin splitting his face.

"I have one of those! Wait right there, I'll go get it and show you," he said to Bobby before he rushed off up the stairs to his room.

Bobby sat there patiently, staring at the TV, his eyebrows furrowed in concentration as he took in what was on-screen while the familiar thud of closet doors opening and slamming shut came from upstairs. Before long, Tommy raced back down holding his small drone and controller aloft like a prize.

"C'mon, let's go!" he exclaimed, grabbing Bobby's paw and hurrying to the front door.

"Hey, just be careful out there you two. It's almost lunchtime so stay close, ok?" Isla called out.

"Yes mom," Tommy's enthusiastic reply drifted back through the already open door.

Isla wheeled herself into the kitchen, opening the blinds on the window overlooking the front yard to keep an eye on Tommy and Bobby. Tommy was kneeling on the soft grass, pointing out the buttons and joysticks on the controller and explaining their function to a curious Bobby.

With a smile, she went about retrieving the cold meats, cheese and spreads that was their standard lunch fare. As she hummed a cheerful tune to herself, the peace was shattered by the violent screeching of tires, the jarring sound of a car braking hard and skidding on the road before her house, accompanied by Tommy's high-pitched, terrified scream. Paralyzing dread coursed through her, a deafening ringing filling her head and constricting her throat, cutting off her breath. It wasn't until she had managed to gasp some air that she realized the high-pitched ringing was her own scream. Her trembling fingers scrambled to coordinate themselves enough to wheel her toward the door, down the makeshift ramp attached, and down the driveway toward the gate that should have been closed but was now wide open.

The harsh smell of burnt rubber emanated from directly ahead, her hands scrambling for purchase on the wheels of her wheelchair as she cried out for Tommy. Frantic, she rolled her wheelchair through the gate, spotting a group huddled over a small figure lying before a vehicle.

"N...No, no, no, no no no no," Isla choked out, each word a desperate plea as a wave of nausea washed over her, the icy fist of fear clenching in her chest.

She shoved her way through the milling crowd, finally reaching Tommy, who lay on the ground, his chest heaving as he gasped for air. A young man, looking to be in his early twenties and likely the driver, knelt beside him, his face pale with fear, trying to speak to him.

"My son, that's my son. What did you do? Did you hit him, is he hurt? Tommy, Tommy baby, are you ok?"

Her words came out in a torrent, her pounding heart felt like it was ready to burst out of her chest.

"I didn't hit him, I swear. I think he's having a panic attack or something. He ran straight out in front of me, and I managed to stop in time, but he just collapsed. It must be shock or something."

"Tommy? Tommy, look at me darling, it's ok. It's going to be ok. Do you have your inhaler with you?"

Tommy's face was ashen, his eyes darting frantically as he gasped for air, each breath a ragged, desperate sound. His neck strained, muscles bulging as he fought to draw in air, the constriction in his throat making each breath a struggle. A silent plea shone in his desperate eyes as they found Isla's, and he shook his head, a tremor running through his whole body.

Panic filled Isla when she realised it would take her too long to retrieve the spare inhaler she kept in the medicine cabinet. It wasn't often that Tommy had a panic attack to the degree that it triggered his asthma and needed his Ventolin. So after his initial few episodes, he had taken to leaving it in his room despite Isla telling him he needed to keep it on him at all times.

Just as she opened her mouth to ask for help, a compact figure squeezed through the onlookers and thrust an inhaler in Tommy's hands. A collective gasp, filled with a mixture of shock and awe, erupted from the group as they stared at the small, furry figure before them.

Bobby clasped his paws around Tommy's trembling hands and brought them toward his lips, holding the inhaler in place while Tommy's fumbling fingers depressed the trigger, and a burst of fine mist flew into his mouth. Another followed and Tommy's heaving, wheezing breaths subsided and began to ease back to their easy, natural rhythm.

Tommy's darting, panicked gaze finally landed on Bobby's large, bulbous eyes, brimming with care and concern. The creature's face softened into a comforting smile as he patted Tommy on the chest.

The crowd watched on in silence, stunned by the events that had just taken place. A few people backed away, making the sign of the cross, their eyes wide with terror as they stared at Bobby. Others stood by, mouths agape, as they tried to process Bobby's presence, while a few watched on in curiosity and wonder.

Isla herself could only watch helplessly, her stomach heavy with despair. She was both grateful for Bobby's quick thinking and actions, but also filled with a deep shame. The weight of her failure pressed down on her; she should have been there to protect her son, but she wasn't capable enough in her condition to be there for him when he needed her most. A wave of sadness washed over her as she saw the love in Tommy's gaze, fixed on his little savior. A crushing sense of inadequacy washed over her, hot tears welling in her eyes before she furiously shook her head and wiped them away. This was no time for self-pity. What was done was done. She needed to be there for him now. She reached down to grab his hand and gave it a squeeze.

"I'm so sorry baby, I wanted to go get your inhaler but there was no way I'd have gotten it in time in this thing." She gestured at the wheelchair with regret.

"I know mommy, it's ok. Bobby saved me."

Tommy pushed himself up on his elbows, then stood, brushing off his clothes. He smiled with a nervous tremor as he looked into the concerned eyes of those surrounding him, before one person knelt before him to meet his eyes.

"I'm so sorry mate, I... I didn't see you until the last minute. I feel horrible. Is there anything I can do?"

"No, it's ok really. It was my fault. My drone ran out of battery, and I saw your car and I thought I had enough time to get it but I didn't. I'm sorry, I didn't mean to scare you."

Rising back to his feet, the young man visibly relaxed, though a worried frown still creased his brow.

"No need to apologize, I'm just glad you're ok."

With a pale, ashen face, Isla gave him a curt nod of acknowledgement before grasping Tommy's hand once more.

"Come on, let's get you inside. I'll make you a hot chocolate. Would you like that?"

With a nod, Tommy grasped Bobby's hand, and the three of them started up the driveway, leaving behind the still shocked murmurs of the crowd behind them as they began to disperse.

Isla ushered Tommy inside and made him sit on a chair, Bobby sitting next to him, his paw still firmly ensconced in Tommy's. As Isla prepared the hot chocolate, she couldn't help but feel a pang of jealousy wash over her as she watched the pair. Bobby patted Tommy's back before Tommy burst into heaving sobs, the impact of the events finally hitting him. Isla stopped what she was doing and wheeled over to him, extending her arms for a hug.

"Hey sweetie, it's ok. It's all over now, everything is fine. You're safe."

Tommy entwined himself in her arms, letting go of Bobby's hand as his small body trembled against her chest, his tears intermingling with hers. Through a haze of her own tears, she glanced over Tommy's shoulder, seeking Bobby's eyes, her heart overflowing with unspoken thanks. Bobby's narrowed eyes, filled with barely suppressed rage, met hers; a chilling expression etched upon his face.

A jolt of shock ran through her, stemming the flow of her tears. Though Bobby had been given to them to assist and help Tommy, it was clear the attachment had grown to a point where the creature was fiercely protective of him. Perhaps dangerously so. It was possible the creature didn't know that Isla, being wheelchair bound, couldn't help Tommy as much as she wanted to. If she could explain that to Bobby, perhaps it would ease the animosity the creature felt for her. She decided to try to explain things to Bobby when she had a chance. As ludicrous as that thought sounded, Bobby had proven to be much more than the pet she and Boyd had expected, possibly even more than the NeuroBalance Institute had expected.

A few minutes of heavy sobbing passed before Tommy pulled away from Isla, his eyes red and puffy, sniffling as he wiped them before turning his attention to Bobby, pulling him into a tight embrace. Isla smiled thinly as she wheeled herself away to finish making the hot chocolate, sneaking glances back at the pair as she did so. Each time, her eyes were met by those of the now blank, unnervingly expressionless ones of Bobby, watching her every move as he rubbed Tommy's back in comfort. She felt an icy shiver of fear run down her back. If she was going to explain things to Bobby, she needed to do it sooner rather than later, before the creature decided that she was an enemy. That was, if it didn't think of her like one already.

Chapter 7
Isla

That chance never came. Time seemed to stretch as Isla, on edge from the day's events, kept a watchful eye on Tommy and Bobby. Though she gave them space, her nerves felt like a tight band around her chest. The pair spent the majority of their time in the lounge room, once again playing card games and perusing cat videos online. Hearing the chuckles of Tommy lifted Isla's spirits somewhat, but her concern and frayed nerves remained.

Her anxiety skyrocketed when things went quiet, and she ducked her head in to see the pair hunched over with the heads together. Tommy was whispering to Bobby and for a second, she could have sworn Bobby was responding with whispers of his own. The whispering died instantly when Bobby saw her, his stare intense, his lips curling into a quick feral snarl before settling into a neutral mask that somehow felt even more unsettling. His huge bulging eyes were conveying far more than his mere expression allowed. There was a primal fury there, an unforgiving look that made her realize no amount of explanation could change his thoughts about her. Tommy noticed Bobby's reaction and studied him before turning his attention to her, his expression troubled, as if he didn't know what to think. She offered a strained smile, then retreated to the kitchen, her entire body trembling with a nervous energy.

Closing her eyes, she tried some deep breathing exercises to calm down her pounding heart. A torrent of chaotic thoughts flooded her mind, each one vying for attention. She wanted to pick up the phone and call Janet to take Bobby away, yet the thought of the potentially devastating impact it would have on Tommy's already strained mental health stopped her cold. Her thoughts raced, thinking of ways of getting Bobby to accept her, but it felt to her like it was too late. There was no way she could take him out on a family outing for bonding time, both because he wasn't a social creature, and it would cause too much chaos when people saw him. She was also under strict instructions not to take him out as the creatures were still under trial and were to be kept out of public knowledge for now. Although given the events of the day, the cat was likely already out of the bag. She decided she would make an effort to include herself in activities with him and Bobby, hoping that, by treating him as family, he would eventually accept her.

Deciding to refresh herself, she wheeled to the base of the stairs, stopping to check in with Tommy and Bobby on the way. Tommy had gotten out his tub of marbles and the pair were taking turns picking out their favourites in preparation for their game ahead.

Reaching for the walking stick leaning against the side of the stairs, she stood up gingerly, wincing when a jolt of pain shot down her hip. With all the events of the day, she had forgotten to do her injury rehabilitation stretches and exercises. Without those, her joints had stiffened and likely caused a recurrence of swelling. She swore silently to herself. As if she didn't have enough to worry about. It had only been two weeks since she'd dislocated her hip. The Doctor had estimated a two-to-three-month recovery. It would be at least another two weeks before she could leave the wheelchair behind, and that was only if she was diligent in doing her physiotherapy routine.

With her hand on the railing, she started up the stairs, just as the sound of clicking marbles and Tommy's gleeful cry filled the air. A smile touched her lips. The fact that Tommy had managed to find joy after what had happened that day was remarkable. It astounded her how children bounced back. If only it were that easy as an adult.

She made it to the top of the stairs and decided to forgo taking the wheelchair waiting for her, opting to hobble to the bathroom instead. After such a long time sitting down, her muscles were crying out for a bit of exercise. After relieving herself she stopped in the bedroom to perform some rudimentary stretches and exercises, groaning as her muscles protested with each movement she made. Making her way back toward the stairs afterwards, she could move a little more freely and felt much better for the small break. She was determined to make the most of the rest of the day and just enjoy Tommy and his new zest for life, putting aside the worries she had about Bobby until later.

Taking the stairs down carefully one step at a time, she pictured herself filling the next hour by unwinding at the kitchen table with a warm cup of coffee and the latest book by her favourite thriller writer. She was so engrossed in her thoughts that she didn't notice the scattered marbles at the foot of the stairs until her foot landed on them and slipped out from under her. Unable to stop herself, she was propelled backwards, landing hard on her back onto the marbles, the back of her head catching the edge of the bottom step with a sickening thud. A blinding flash of pain shot from the point of impact, her vision going dark as waves of agony pulsed from her head to her feet. A groan escaped her lips as she touched the back of her head; the sticky warmth of blood was unmistakable. Black spots swam before her eyes, a nauseating ringing assaulting her ears, making her fight desperately to hold on to consciousness.

Through the blurry haze of her vision, a small, indistinct shape appeared and loomed above her, bending down as if to examine her. The figure snapped into sharp focus for a heartbeat, its features briefly clear before fading back into the blurry obscurity. It was Bobby. The small creature darted away at the approach of Tommy's small, thudding footsteps as his faint, panicked cries barely pierced through the ringing in her ears.

The black spots faded from her vision, only to be replaced by a wave of dizziness and intense nausea, causing her to roll onto her side and vomit. Taking deep, ragged breaths, she closed her eyes trying to steady her vision. She felt the small hands of Tommy as he tugged at her shoulder, his small frantic cries causing her to roll herself onto her back and open her eyes to meet his distraught, tear-streaked gaze.

"I... I'm ok sweetheart," she managed, squinting her eyes against the daylight that suddenly felt far too bright.

"Mommy, I love you mommy. I'm sorry, I'm sorry, it was my fault. I didn't mean for this to happen, I'm sorry," he sobbed as he collapsed on top of her.

"It's ok, baby. I'll be ok. I just need a few minutes, ok? Then I'll get right back up."

Tommy lifted his head from her chest and looked at her with tear-stained cheeks, his glistening eyes filled with resolve.

"I'll help you mommy; I'll get you a band-aid. I'll be right back."

Without waiting for her to answer, he sprang to his feet and headed for the first-aid cabinet, yanking it open. A chaotic jumble of supplies tumbled to the floor as he searched, before he finally found the box of Band-Aids and retrieved one from it before returning to present it to her triumphantly.

"Here you are mommy, this will fix you right up," he said, placing it into her hand.

"Thanks sweetheart," she whispered, her eyelids fluttering as she fought to stay awake.

"I'll get you some water, just stay there," he said, his earnest smile touching her heart despite the pain. When he returned with the water, she carefully propped herself on her elbows, fighting the dizziness with each movement but eventually succeeding. After taking a few sips, she started to feel a little better, her vision slowly losing its haziness until it was once again clear.

"Thank sweetie," she said gratefully, handing him back the cup. He nodded happily and trotted off back to the kitchen to put the cup in the sink.

Performing each action carefully, she rose from the floor to her feet, almost falling back to the floor as she swayed drunkenly before finding the stair railing to stabilize herself against. She reached for the back of her head, wincing in pain as she felt the sticky, warm blood matting her hair. Leaning heavily against the wall, she made her way to the first-aid cabinet, opening it and scanning its contents for a bandage.

She had to wait for Boyd to come home before she could see a doctor. In the meantime, a bandage would have to make do. To her dismay, she found it wasn't in there. She looked down at the scattered supplies on the floor and spotted it at the entrance to the kitchen. The bandage lay at the base of Bobby's large furry paws, his expression a mixture of satisfaction and malicious glee as he stared at her. His wet nose was twitching, his mouth slightly parted in a smile revealing his pointed teeth, exposing them on purpose as he shifted his gaze from her to the small puddle of blood behind her where she had landed and hit her head on the floor. His face slackened, his thin tongue flicking out, a silent testament to the intense longing reflected in his hungry eyes.

The way he reacted was identical to his response to Tommy's injury — a chillingly familiar pattern of heightened alertness, twitching muscles, and an almost imperceptible change in the way his fur stood on end. Only this time, he displayed undisguised desire.

"I'll get it mommy," Tommy said, following the direction of Isla's gaze toward the bandage.

"Don't you want the band-aid?"

She looked from the creature to him, drawn by the worry in his voice.

"Sorry sweetie, I think my cut might be a bit too big for a band-aid."

With a nod of understanding, he walked to the bandage and picked it up, handing it to her before turning back to face Bobby.

He laughed upon seeing Bobby's face, still lit up with desire and staring at the blood behind Isla, "Bobby, what's wrong with your face? You're so funny," he said, shaking his head.

"Will you be ok Mommy? Do you need anything else?" He asked, turning back to face Isla.

"Can you and Bobby please pick up the marbles? Daddy will be home soon, and we don't want him to fall and get hurt like me, do we?" she said, pointing to the back of her head with a pained smile.

"No, we don't," he said gravely.

"I'm sorry Mommy, I don't know how the marbles got down there, we were playing in the lounge room. Bobby dropped some of his but he picked them up."

"It's ok baby, when Daddy gets home, we'll get this all sorted, and Mommy will be back to normal in no time, ok?"

With a tight-lipped, concerned smile, Tommy nodded, his eyes conveying his worry.

"Come on Bobby, let's clean these marbles up."

He tugged Bobby toward the marbles scattered in the hall near the stairs as Isla moved toward the kitchen, using the wall to steady herself, the bandage in the other hand.

As she neared the kitchen, the familiar sound of the front door opening announced Boyd's arrival; his heavy footsteps pounded across the floor, the door shutting behind him with a thud.

"Good timing," Isla said weakly, as he strode into the kitchen. Feeling her legs wobbling beneath her, she stumbled towards the kitchen table.

"Isla? Oh my god, are you alright?"

Boyd dropped his bag of tools to the floor with a loud metallic thud and rushed toward Isla, throwing her arm over his shoulder to take her weight and guide her toward a chair.

"What happened? God, you're bleeding. We need to get you to the hospital."

She shook her head weakly.

"I slipped on some marbles and hit my head on the stairs, I'll be ok. We can't afford it. I'll be fine. I just need you to clean the wound and bandage it up."

"No way. I'm taking you to the hospital. We can't take a chance with something like this. We'll worry about the money later."

"No, I..." She began to protest, the words forming on her lips, but then she caught herself. Boyd was right. Head injuries shouldn't be taken lightly, and hers felt particularly nasty. Guilt flooded through her at the thought of the bill that would be awaiting them at the end. She could feel tears welling up once again. She felt utterly spent, both physically and mentally. The stress of watching over Tommy and keeping a close eye on Bobby. Her guilt about the accident and her inability to help Tommy when he needed it most. And now her accident, which judging by the look that she had seen on Bobby's face, was likely not an accident at all, was just too much for her to handle, and wracking sobs began to shake her body, intensifying the pain from her head wound.

She leaned into Boyd, letting the tears flow. She felt useless, a burden to both Boyd and Tommy. It felt as though her life was crumbling around her like a sandcastle hit by a wave, and she was powerless to stop it.

"Hey, it's ok. It'll be ok," Boyd whispered, holding her close against him, rocking her slowly.

"C'mon, let's go."

"What about Tommy and Bobby?"

A grimace crossed Boyd's face. Bobby and his reception at the hospital hadn't crossed his mind, but they had no other option.

"It's ok, we'll put a jacket or hoodie over him or something. We'll work it out when we get there. I'll go get your wheelchair. Where is it?"

Isla blinked, trying to think through the fog of pain and frowned, realizing that the wheelchair hadn't been where she had left it at the base of the stairs.

"I... I don't know... I could have sworn I left it at the base of the stairs... I..."

"It's ok, it can't be far. I'll be back in a sec."

Chapter 8

Tommy

Tommy stood in the middle of the hallway leading toward the stairs, staring at the scattered marbles in confusion.

"I really don't understand how these got here."

He stopped, the memory of their marble tournament flooding back, his eyes widening as only one explanation came to mind. During their game, Bobby had dropped his container of marbles, and they had rolled toward the entrance leading to the base of the stairs and chased after them. He had come back with the container rattling in his paw, so he'd assumed he'd collected them all.

"Bobby, did you forget to pick these up?"

Bobby hung his head, one foot tracing a tile on the floor, a picture of shame. He nodded slowly in guilt.

"Oh Bobby." Tommy sighed, shaking his head in disappointment, a deep frown etched onto his face.

"You have to make sure you pick up everything if you drop things, ok? Mommy has always taught me that, so we need to make sure we follow that rule from now on."

Bobby looked up, meeting his gaze nervously, his eyes filled with sorrow and regret and nodded once more.

"OK, now let's pick all these up and pack them away."

He stopped, his eyes catching sight of the pool of blood at the foot of the stairs and the vomit nearby.

"We should clean that up too. But just looking at it is making me sick. Do you... Do you think you can clean it up for me?"

Bobby nodded energetically, his sudden enthusiasm startling Tommy who looked at him in surprise.

"Ok, the paper towels and spray are in the kitchen cupboard under the sink. You clean that up and I'll pick up the..." Tommy stopped, his mouth agape in horror.While Tommy was still talking, Bobby had thrown himself towards the pool of blood, his tongue extending toward the sticky crimson liquid. He curled his tongue to lap up the congealing liquid, then retracted it with a sickening slurp. He leaned back, eyes closed, a slight tremor of excitement making his nose twitch. His lips curled into a small, satisfied smile, the muscles in his leathery angular face transforming into a look of pure, unadulterated bliss.

"Bobby no! What are you doing?"

Bobby ignored him and opened his eyes, a look of what could only be burning desire transforming his face from a once friendly and open countenance to that of the animalistic side it had been created from, its purpose now singular. To satisfy his urges to the detriment of all else. With a wet, rasping snuffle, he lowered his head, coating his tongue with the viscous crimson liquid, his teeth clicking and grinding with an almost frantic energy, as if the taste wasn't enough. His movements were quick and desperate, fuelled by a bloodlust that Tommy's calls to him couldn't pierce.

Tommy could only watch on in horror, his body frozen as he watched his pet, his friend, which had brought him joy and comfort in such a short time frame, transform his behaviour into something terrifyingly unfamiliar to him. It felt like a piece of him was breaking off, the sharp sting of loss adding to the year's unbearable burden of sadness and confusion.

Tears streamed down his face as he continued to watch his friend devour his mother's blood until there was just a small streak left, before that too was lapped up.

Tommy stared at the rapidly breathing hunched figure of Bobby, the creature still lost in the ecstasy of finding what it had unknowingly desired since it was first created.

Disgusted and disappointed both, Tommy turned his back on him and began to pick up the spilled marbles. The familiar feeling of numbness began to sweep over him, his brain's self-defence mechanism kicking in to try and protect him from the big feelings that were starting to build within from the events of the day and what he had just witnessed. First, Bobby's show of animosity toward his mom in the lounge room earlier in the day while he was talking to him about the bullying that shaped his life, and now this. It was simply too much to bear.

Chapter 9

Boyd

Boyd's mind raced as he headed toward the hallway beyond the kitchen. He flitted from worrying about Isla, to how the accident occurred, to Tommy and Bobby, to money, and then back to getting Isla to the hospital, finally settling on focusing only on that and dealing with the rest later.

Entering the hallway, he saw Tommy picking up something that looked like a marble, while Bobby panted heavily by the stairs.

"Tommy, have you seen mommy's wheelchair? It should be right there next to the stairs."

Boyd pointed toward the alcove between the stairs and the wall.

Tommy looked at the space where the wheelchair should be and shook his head.

Tommy's silence caused Boyd to pause and study him, concern morphing into dread as he took in Tommy's familiar impassive face. It was the face he had worn most of the year before Bobby had arrived in their lives. Tommy's eyes turned to fix on the stiffened form of Bobby, still hunched over and breathing heavily. A frown creased Boyd's brow as his gaze flickered between Bobby and Tommy, the silence heavy with unspoken tension.

"Hey, did something happen between you two?" Boyd inquired softly, crouching down next to Tommy. His heart sank at the lack of response. Tommy was still intently watching Bobby, his gaze unwavering. He was close enough now to see a slight sheen of sweat on Tommy's forehead. Boyd lifted his hand to Tommy's forehead, to check his temperature but instead found his skin cold and clammy.

Something had definitely happened, but he couldn't afford to try and work it out right now, he needed to find the wheelchair and get Isla to the hospital. He scanned the area and noticed the congealing puddle of vomit near the stairs, making a mental note to clean it up later when they got back. Out of the corner of his eye, he saw the tip of the handlebars through the doorway next to the stairs leading to the lounge room. With a sigh of relief, he grabbed hold of them and wheeled it back toward the kitchen, looking back over his shoulder at Tommy.

"Tommy, can you go and dig out one of your Halloween masks from upstairs and a hoodie or jacket? We need to take Mommy to hospital and don't want people to be worried about seeing Bobby. He'll have to wear them when we get there."

He tore his gaze from Bobby, gave a sharp nod of acknowledgement, then ran past the still figure up the stairs to his room.

Boyd refocused his attention back to the task at hand. A few minutes later, the family was on the way to the hospital, the car silent except for the small whimpers of pain from Isla. He couldn't shake the feeling that something terrible and irreversible had happened. A deep foreboding settled in his mind as he glanced between the pained expression on Isla's face to the statuesque body language of Tommy in the rearview mirror and to the silent and disconnected presence of Bobby.

A stony resolve settled into his mind. Once Isla was seen to and settled back home, he would get to the bottom of what had happened. If it was anything to do with Bobby, he would make it clear to Janet and the NeuroBalance Institute that he was a failure and needed to be removed from their home.

Chapter 10

Isla

Pulling up outside the emergency entrance of the hospital, Boyd got out to pull out Isla's wheelchair while she leaned back in the passenger seat, taking in deep breaths to steady her swimming vision. She felt almost certain at this point that she had a concussion. She caught sight of the two boys sitting rigidly in the backseat in the rearview mirror, the silence thick between them, and frowned. It was hard enough to stay conscious, let alone try to make sense of their peculiar behaviour.

It wasn't long before the passenger door opened to the sight of her wheelchair awaiting her, and Boyd's arms, ready to welcome her into his steady grasp. Gingerly moving so as not to trigger a blackout, she inched herself to the edge of her seat and reached out to grip onto Boyd. Supporting her weight, he shifted her into the chair and positioned her feet onto the rests before opening the backdoor to let Tommy and Bobby out.

"Come on boys, we need to go. Tommy, can you help Bobby with the mask and hoodie?"

Boyd released the brakes on the wheelchair and waited impatiently for the pair to emerge from the vehicle. Isla watched the interaction between Tommy and Bobby dreamily from outside as Tommy hesitated, looking down at the basic plastic wolf mask on top of the hoodie on his lap, and then back up at Bobby.

Bobby sat there silently, looking out the window next to him, his nose, ears and facial expression completely still. Slowly unbuckling himself, Tommy shifted toward Bobby, slipping the hoodie on his stiffened form before placing and positioning the mask carefully over his face.

Bobby turned his head slowly toward Tommy, a distant curiosity evident in his eyes through the holes in the mask. Tommy's lips twitched at the absurd sight before him; a giggle escaped, before turning into a torrent of laughter as Bobby just sat there staring, his expression unreadable.

Something had changed in Bobby's demeanor since her accident, but she just couldn't think straight through the pain and fogginess to decipher what it was. A few moments later, Tommy and Bobby emerged from the car, and she was wheeled with haste towards the hospital entrance before everything fell into darkness.

She awoke to a bright beam of light shining into her eyes, followed by sharp pangs of pain shooting down her spine from the wound at the back of her head, as her body adjusted itself to wakefulness.

"Welcome back," a voice from the blurry figure before her said, as it stepped back.

Blinking her eyes to clear the black spots dancing in her vision from her sudden wakening, she squinted and focused with effort on the source of the voice. The smiling face of a man in a white coat gradually came into focus, the nametag 'Doctor Julius Preston' pinned to his lapel.

The Doctor turned his attention from her to the worried face of Boyd, who sat fidgeting on a chair nearby.

"She will be fine. She has a stage two concussion and her head will be very tender for a while, but there will be no lasting damage. I'll get the wound tended to and bandaged by one of our lovely nurses here. It will need to be changed daily for four to five days. I'll also send you home with some painkillers."

He redirected his attention to her.

"You are going to have to take it easy for at least the next week. Bed rest as much as possible for the next one to two days or longer if you still feel dizzy."

Isla opened her mouth to protest, her mind struggling to find the words.

"But Doctor, I can't. I have to look after Tommy and Bobby."

The Doctor looked at the two boys sitting next to Boyd with a grimace before turning to Boyd.

"Is it possible for you to stay home while Isla recovers?"

"I wish I could, doc," Boyd sighed, his eyes cast downward.

"Unfortunately, we really don't have much money and since Isla can't work, I have to if we want to stay afloat."

He rubbed his sweaty hands off on his jeans before he continued, "I'll try to leave as early as I can. If I work through lunch and start earlier, I can come back a couple of hours early, but that's going to be the best I can do."

"Well then, I guess you two are going to have to look after yourselves for a little while. Are you up to the challenge?" the Doctor queried, crossing his arms over his chest as he looked with feigned seriousness at Tommy and Bobby.

Tommy nodded, his face settling into a look of determination which made all three of them smile. He raised his hand in a mock salute, his hand catching the bottom of Bobby's mask and sending it tumbling to the floor.

The Doctor gasped, his face paling as he stared with wide eyes at Bobby.

Bobby sat there unmoving, returning the doctor's gaze with an inquisitive look, as if studying his reaction, before a subtle smile touched his lips.

"What... What is that?" The doctor whispered.

"Oh, um, yeah about that," Boyd chuckled nervously.

"Bobby here is an experimental pet, a mental health assistant for Tommy," he paused at the look of shock that took shape on the doctor's face, before he continued quickly.

"The NeuroBalance Institute developed him as part of a new trial for kids who have been through trauma and suffer severe psychological effects. He is meant to help out Tommy by being a constant companion that will raise his spirits in any way he can."

"I... I see," the doctor said, regaining his composure, his face still pale.

"Well, I'm sure he's doing just that, right Tommy?"

Tommy's eyes flickered to Bobby before darting back down to the floor; a small nod was his only response.

Swivelling in his chair, Dr. Julius faced his computer monitor, keyed in some information on Isla's record, and picked up the phone, glancing back at Isla.

"Let me just get a nurse to get that wound fixed up for you."

With a push of a button, the doctor connected to the nurse's station and quickly arranged for one. Setting down the phone, he turned back to face them, looking pointedly at Boyd.

"Boyd, can I speak to you outside for a moment?"

"Sure doc," he rested a hand on Isla's shoulder and gave it a squeeze before following the doctor out the door.

Chapter 11

Boyd

Closing the door softly behind him, Doctor Julius moved down the corridor a little, peering at the door before speaking.

"That creature. Bobby, is it?" Without waiting for Boyd's reply, he continued, "Do you know what species of animals it is derived from by any chance?"

Boyd paused as a nurse rounded the corner and headed toward the consultation room. He and the doctor acknowledged her with a nod before she entered. He frowned as he struggled to recall what was in the information booklet given to them.

"I believe it was part bat, part cat and part dog, but each part heavily modified and enhanced to give it enough intelligence to read and recognise the different emotions of the person it is assigned to."

The doctor nodded thoughtfully; his forehead creased with worry.

"I thought so. Given the creature's facial features, I would say the bat part isn't just any bat. It has the features of a vampire bat. You can see it in the snub nose, the wide eyes, the teeth and its ears and, I'd also wager, its claws."

"Is that a problem?" Boyd said, his brow furrowed in confusion.

"It very well might be. You see, I would surmise that the reason the NeuroBalance Institute used the vampire bat in this case is because they are very social creatures and form bonds with each other. Given the mix of cat and dog along with the vampire bat, the bond they form with their assigned owner would be very, very strong. This isn't an issue in and of itself, but it could mean that the creature would be very protective and put its owner above everyone else, possibly even harming those it felt threatened the wellbeing of its owner."

The doctor paused, stroking his chin thoughtfully, then continued.

"It also might mean it has an attraction to blood. It wasn't obviously noticeable, but there were small telltale signs it is at least interested, judging by the way it was twitching its nose and ears a little. Now it could also be that it is agitated by the unfamiliar environment and my presence, but I would be cautious going forward."

He noticed Boyd's mounting worry and sighed.

"Look, all I'm saying is that you should try and keep a close eye on this creature. Being experimental, it could have unexpected behavioural issues and potentially be dangerous."

Boyd's face was pallid when he replied.

"It can speak Doc. Isla heard it say 'Bedbug' plain as day last night. Not only that, but I could have sworn it was spying on us last night when we were discussing it."

The doctor's jaw dropped in surprise; shock written across his face.

"Listen, I might be being overly cautious here, but I would suggest you get the creature removed immediately. This behaviour is unnatural and I'm sure, not what was intended."

"We can't, Doc, my son Tommy. He's.... He's only just come out of his shell. He hasn't spoken in six months and since Bobby has come along, he's come back to us.

If we remove Bobby suddenly, there's no telling what will happen to him."

Boyd let out a heavy, defeated sigh before he continued, "We have an appointment with Janet from the NeuroBalance Institute in two days to see if anything can be done. If not, we will have to get him removed. But I dread what that will do to Tommy."

The doctor's frown softened into a nod as he took in Boyd's words.

"I understand. It's a delicate situation. Just please, look after yourselves and keep an eye out on Bobby. Please do try to get back early if you have to work tomorrow. Given Isla's current state and the situation with Bobby, it will be tough for her to handle things on her own."

"I definitely will Doc. Thank you for your help and giving me the heads-up about Bobby."

Acknowledging him with a nod, the doctor headed back towards the consultation room with Boyd in tow, worry written on his face.

Chapter 12

Isla

By the time the doctor and Boyd returned, and the nurse had finished cleaning and bandaging her wound, Isla had started to feel better. Despite the persistent pounding in her head, her swimming vision had steadied, which offered some relief from the nausea.

As the pain receded, she was able to reflect on what had happened when she had slipped and fell. The image of Bobby's creepy smile was burnt into her mind. She had no doubt he was behind the marbles scattered in her path; the question was what she was going to do about it? She chewed on her fingernails as Boyd wheeled her back down the hall toward the exit. She could feel Bobby's eyes boring into the back of her head from behind, where he and Tommy were trailing her. With Boyd working the next day and her supposed to be confined to the bed, how was she supposed to ensure that Tommy would be safe? Was it just her that Bobby had a problem with or was he going to turn on Tommy too? She didn't think so, but she couldn't deny there was a distance between the pair now. Had something else happened while she was nearly incapacitated?

She sighed, feeling her anxiety build up to a crescendo. That and the pulsating pain from the back of her head had combined to form the beginnings of a migraine, or at the very least, an intense headache. She needed to close her eyes for a while. At least with Boyd back, she could get some rest and hopefully be able to face tomorrow's challenges from her wheelchair rather than the bed, despite the doctor's orders.

Boyd wheeled her out of the hospital towards their car in the nearby emergency parking lot just as the sun was setting and casting its last rays. A chill had set in as it had the last few nights, signalling the oncoming end of fall. The wheels of the wheelchair crushed the still crisp and freshly fallen leaves of the maple leaves carpeting the path along the side of the hospital leading to the car park. A swirling breeze whipped through the branches of the trees high above the slope across from the hospital, rustling the leaves and sending a shower of them drifting down. Tommy, delighted, ran past to catch them, his hands outstretched. The small, furry form of Bobby ran after him, holding his paws out, emulating Tommy.

Seeing Tommy play, albeit in a more subdued fashion than what he had when he had first come out of his shell, brought a soft smile to Isla's face, yet a hint of sadness lingered in her eyes. After the day's events, her heart was more set on removing Bobby from their household. It worried her no end as to what it would do to Tommy, but it had to be done for the safety of them all.

Reaching the car, Boyd eased her inside and began to pack away the wheelchair. Closing her eyes in relief and leaning her head against the cool leather of the headrest, she found herself drifting off. She was fast asleep by the time Boyd pulled out of the carpark and headed for home.

Chapter 13

Boyd

The glow of the headlights revealed the leaf-laden driveway as Boyd turned into it. Another job for the weekend ahead, he thought to himself with a small sigh. It wasn't until they reached the garage that he realized that they weren't alone. There was a figure, shrouded in shadows, leaning against the pillar near the front door, the telltale red glow of the cigarette it was holding, punctuating the darkness with intermittent flickers.

"Wait here," Boyd threw over his shoulder as he opened the car door, a scowl twisting his features as he exited and approached the figure.

"Who are you, and what the hell do you want?"

"Whoa, hold on there big guy, I'm a friend, I swear," the man said. He tightened the cinch of his trench coat, bending down to extinguish his cigarette on the ground before extending his hand.

"Jonathan Murloch, reporter for The Urban Echo newspaper. I just wanted to ask you about your little creature you have here. I hear it was quite the saviour today."

"I don't know what the hell you're talking about. Now, if you'll excuse me, I need to get my wife inside and up to bed."

Jonathan narrowed his eyes in suspicion, "Why? What happened? Did the creature do something? Is it dangerous?"

"Please leave us alone, Mr Murloch. None of us have any intention of talking to you. You're wasting your time here."

"I just want a few words, that's all," Jonathan said, stepping closer.

"We all want something Mr Murloch. Right now, I want you off my property before I call the cops. You have five seconds."

"But I..."

"5....4...."

"Ok, Ok, I'm going."

Jonathan reached into his pocket, producing a card.

"Here, in case you or your wife change your mind."

He offered the card to Boyd. A few seconds later, when he realized that Boyd wasn't going to take it, he moved back toward the door and left the card leaning against the wall.

Boyd stared icily at Jonathan as he retreated, heading toward a van parked on the opposite side of the road. He waited until the van had disappeared around the corner before returning to the car, where Isla remained fast asleep. He winced at the thought of waking her, but he had no choice.

Opening the door, he put a hand on her shoulder and shook her gently.

"Hey honey, we're home. Let's get you inside, hey?"

Isla stirred and opened her eyes, the car's overhead light making her wince.

"Is everything ok?" she whispered with a pained frown, lifting her hand to massage her forehead with a groan.

"Yeah, we're home. We need to get you into bed, sweetheart."

"Ok," she said, nodding gingerly.

He retrieved her wheelchair from the back of the Land Rover and carefully helped her into it, just as Bobby and Tommy got out of the car. A huge yawn escaped Tommy's lips as he stretched, his limbs cracking; Bobby, fascinated, copied him.

With Isla in her wheelchair, Boyd pushed her toward the door, stopping to pick up the card and shoving it into his pocket without thinking. He unlocked the door, flipped on the lights, and wheeled her toward the stairs.

"Ok boys, time to get ready for bed. I'll come say goodnight when I get your mom settled."

"Ok, daddy," Tommy said, before he and Bobby dashed past them and up the stairs. Bobby sped ahead of Tommy who stopped abruptly, changing course to run back down to kiss Isla on the cheek goodnight before returning to meet Bobby at the top.

Boyd stopped the wheelchair at the foot of the stairs and helped Isla to stand, passing her the walking stick from its holder. Isla leaned on him as they slowly climbed the stairs and walked down the hall to their bedroom.

By the time they got there, Isla was exhausted and barely able to keep her eyes open. He sat her on the bed and helped her shuffle under the covers; her trembling hand reaching out to grasp his.

"Boyd, I... I need to tell you something, Bobby he... he is dangerous... we need to... the safe word... Fer..." her voice faded into silence as she fell into a deep, exhausted sleep.

Boyd looked down at her, frowning thoughtfully. He had been so consumed with getting Isla to the hospital that he hadn't spared much thought about how the accident had happened.

His thoughts drifted back to when he had first seen Isla when he arrived home. According to her, she had slipped on some marbles and hit her head on the stairs.

His frown deepened when he recalled the two boys in the hallway when he had gone to retrieve the wheelchair. He had seen Tommy pick up a marble from the floor while Bobby had been near the base of the stairs. What had Bobby been doing there? Unlike Tommy, he didn't have any marbles in his hand, he was just there hunched over, his rapid breathing hinting at exertion or excitement. Was he curious about the scene of the accident, about the vomit nearby? His thoughts turned to Isla's wound. Judging by the amount of blood matting the back of her head, he should have seen traces on the stairs or floor tiles, but he couldn't recall any when he had gone to retrieve the wheelchair.

It was possible Tommy had cleaned it up before he got there but he didn't recall seeing any cleaning supplies nearby, nor any paper towels or a washcloth.

A sudden suspicion sparked in his mind, recalling the doctor's words at the hospital, his eyes widening in alarm at the implications. Releasing his hand from Isla's limp grip, he gently patted her hand, tucking the blankets around her before quietly heading back down the dimly lit hallway to the stairs, descending them slowly. Switching on the hallway lights, he scanned the floor and last few carpeted stairs, searching for any signs of blood. As he had suspected, there were some damp patches on the last step, but no trace at all on the tiles in the hallway. He felt a sickening lurch in his stomach as the horrifying truth dawned: Bobby had cleaned it, but it wasn't with any cleaning supplies.

Chapter 14

Tommy

Having kissed his mother's cheek, Tommy bounded up the stairs, his racing heart a testament to both his effort and the eventful day. The familiar numb feeling that had plagued him since the events of the winter earlier in the year was on the verge of taking over once more. It felt like he was lost at sea during a particularly violent storm; the waves battering him from all sides and he was struggling to stay afloat, but he could feel himself tiring, succumbing to its ferocity.

It all stemmed from Bobby. Bobby, who had freed him from the emotional black hole he had been swept into and who now threatened to cast him back in once more. He needed to find out if Bobby had put the marbles there on purpose to hurt mommy. He needed to understand why Bobby had lapped up her blood. He knew some animals behaved that way, but this had felt more sinister somehow.

He rushed through his bedtime routine, getting changed and brushing his teeth with Bobby by his side as usual, wanting to wait until they got into bed before he mentioned anything.

Finally, when they were both under the covers in their beds, he shifted, turning onto his side nervously so he could face him.

"Bobby, I need to ask you something," he said, a knot of tension tightening in his stomach.

Bobby turned his head toward him, offering him a tight-lipped smile that didn't reach his eyes. In the soft glow of the lamplight, they almost looked menacing. Tommy felt a shiver, like an icy wave, washing over him, raising goosebumps on his exposed forearms.

"Did... Did you leave the marbles near the stairs on purpose?"

Bobby stiffened, his eyes unblinking and fixed on Tommy, the air thick with tension.

"Answer me Bobby, did you? Did you hurt mommy on purpose?"

Bobby broke off eye contact to look down, a look akin to shame appearing on his face. He nodded slowly, looking back up at Tommy, eyes brimming with genuine sorrow.

Tommy's heart immediately sank and with a sob, he scrambled out from under the covers and ran from the room, tears streaming down his face right as Boyd stepped inside.

"Hey mate, hey, it's ok. Mommy will be ok," he whispered, misconstruing Tommy's tears.

Sobbing, Tommy ran into Boyd's embrace, his body shaking with emotion. It felt like his whole world was falling apart, and he didn't understand why. He just wanted to run away from everything, feel happy and safe like he used to. Sobs continued to wrack his body, and he lost himself in the comfort of Boyd's embrace. There he found the solace he was craving, and the horrors of the day gradually began to fade away.

Chapter 15

Boyd

Boyd held Tommy close, his own tears blurring his vision. He felt helpless, a dull ache settling in his bones. It felt like his heart was being wrenched in two, held together only by the thinnest of stitches. His family was falling apart in front of him and there was nothing he could do about it. Visions of Bobby filled his memories, of him crouching down at the foot of the stairs where Isla's blood should have been, and the path forward suddenly became very clear. They needed to get rid of the creature, and they needed it done as soon as possible. As soon as he returned to the bedroom, he would call Janet and tell her to pick up the failed experiment tomorrow.

Minutes passed before Tommy's heaving sobs turned to sniffles and he pulled away, his innocent tear streaked face melting Boyd's heart. He rested his hands on Tommy's shoulder and looked at him with all the reassurance he could muster.

"I promise everything will be ok mate. Daddy will fix everything, but you have to promise me one thing, ok? Can you be brave for me, just for one more day? Help mommy until Daddy comes back from work tomorrow? Can you do that for me?"

Over Tommy's shoulder, he could just glimpse Bobby's openly jealous gaze staring at them. With a face as hard as granite, Boyd locked his gaze onto Bobby's, the warning clear in the icy depths of his eyes. Bobby's frown deepened, his jaw tight, as he refocused on Tommy, who was looking up at Boyd and giving him a determined nod, his eyes gleaming with resolve.

"Good boy, I'm so very proud of you," Boyd said with a smile, ruffling his curly hair playfully.

A worried, tender smile flickered across Tommy's face before he turned back to his bed, pointedly avoiding Bobby's judgmental stare.

"Goodnight boys," Boyd said with a warm smile directed toward Tommy before he eased the door closed. He headed downstairs to clean up the vomit. Afterwards, he retrieved the information booklet on Bobby, scanning it for Janet's phone number. Finding it, he tapped it into his phone and retreated to the kitchen before making the call.

He leant over the kitchen counter, tapping his fingers on its marble surface as he waited. With each successive ring, his frustration grew. He checked his watch: the luminous green numbers, "11:07 pm", glowed faintly. A sigh escaped his lips as the phone's ring gave way to a flat, automated voice asking him to leave a message.

"Janet, it's Boyd O'Halloran. Look, I know we have an appointment for Thursday but we need you to come and collect Bobby as soon as possible. It's become evident that he just isn't the right fit for us here and, quite frankly, we suspect he might be dangerous. We can't risk having something like that here with our son. Please call as soon as you get this message." He thumbed the end call button and laid the phone down, leaning both forearms on the counter, resting his forehead between them as he took some deep breaths. He had done everything he could. He just had to hope that tomorrow would be incident free, and Janet would turn up to pick up Bobby. Maybe he should have told her to wait until he was back. No, it needed to be done as soon as possible for the safety of his family.

Worry coiled in his stomach like a snake, its grip tightening as his thoughts spiralled. He had a feeling sleep wouldn't come easy tonight, if it even came at all.

Chapter 16

Isla

Isla woke up with a start, feeling a lancing pain emanating from her wound. She opened her eyes slowly, wincing at the blazing sunlight that was just visible from the gaps in-between the curtain and window. She rolled over with a groan, extending her arms to reach for the familiar comfort of Boyd's warmth beside her, but found his side of the bed empty. Judging by the coolness of the sheets on his side, he had been gone a while. She rolled back to her side of the bed, and stared upwards at the ceiling, taking a few deep breaths to try to steady the pounding pain rushing down through the back of her head and clear the fogginess. After a few minutes, she inched herself up to a sitting position, reaching for her phone on the bedside table, which lay face down.

She picked it up, her eyes widening in alarm at the sight of the time: 12:13 pm.

"Oh shit, Tommy must be so hungry," she muttered in dismay, leaning the back of her head on the cool metal of the headboard, savouring the feeling through the warmth of the bandage covering her wound.

The sound of Tommy's laughter drifted through the doorway from downstairs and she sighed in relief, feeling her tense shoulders loosen a little. It sounded like Tommy was doing just fine. With luck, the next few hours before Boyd returned from work would pass by without an issue.

Checking her phone again, she saw she had some missed calls from Janet and a text message.

'Hi Isla, please give me a call as soon as you can. This is a matter of urgency.'

"About damn time you responded," Isla muttered with a yawn. She would deal with it later; first, she needed to check on Tommy and make sure lunch was taken care of.

With a pained grunt, she swung her legs over the side of the bed and stood up gingerly. Picking up the walking stick leaning against the bedside table, she limped to the bathroom to relieve herself. Afterwards, as she stood before the bathroom mirror to study herself, she spotted a sticky note Boyd had attached in the middle of the mirror, so obvious she couldn't miss it. She peeled it from the mirror, a smile spreading across her face as she read it.

'Hey babe, I hope you feel better. I will be back at 2:30pm. Give me a call if you need me before then. Love you XXX.'

She knew, without a shadow of a doubt, how incredibly fortunate she was to have Boyd in her life. The pair had met twelve years ago in Isla's Pilates class she was running at the time at Fit Factory. As a young, fit Pilates instructor, she was well aware of the admiring glances and lingering stares from the men in her classes, many of whom were clearly there for more than just a workout. But there had been one amongst them that she had initially dismissed as just another one of those seedy men that wasn't just showing up; he was attentive and actively involved in every class. Though he had been eyeing her like most of the other guys, he had never approached her or tried to flirt with her. Eventually, her curiosity piqued, she had approached him to engage him in a conversation about the class, and the pair had quickly hit it off. She found him funny and quirky, and his Irish accent only added to his charm. From there, the pair had never looked back. He had always been her rock, the one she could always rely on, her best friend.

Lost in the comforting memories, she brushed her teeth and splashed some cold water over her face. Despite the pain from her wound, she was feeling much better after sleeping in.

Grabbing the handheld mirror from the cabinet, she positioned it behind her head and looked in the mirror to study the bandage. There was a small patch of dried blood that had soaked a section of the bandage. It was in need of a change, but it could wait until after lunch. She glanced at her watch; it was 12:35 p.m. Speaking of lunch, it was past time. She was surprised Tommy hadn't barged into the room to ask her about it yet.

Putting on her silk robe with difficulty, she limped to the bedroom door, toward the wheelchair positioned there, wincing as pain shot up her hip. The fall definitely hadn't helped matters with her injury. Hopefully, it was just a bruise as the nurse had indicated and there was no further damage to her existing injury. She slid her walking stick into its holder, eased herself into the wheelchair with a relieved sigh and rolled down the hallway toward the stairs, thinking about what to make for lunch. Perhaps she could make chicken soup, one of Tommy's favourites, although in her current condition, maybe she needed to keep things simple. Peanut butter sandwiches were always a favourite of Tommy's. While not particularly nutritious, it was probably the most she could manage given her condition.

She was nearing the top of the stairs, still so preoccupied with the thought of lunch that she didn't hear the sudden rush of soft footsteps rushing toward her from the storeroom opposite, until the wheelchair was suddenly given a violent shove, propelling her onto the stairs.

With a cry of terror, she reached out with a desperate hand, her fingers trembling as they grasped the cold metal brake lever above the rear wheels. With a swift and urgent motion, she yanked the lever back, feeling the resistance in her muscles and the click of the lock snapping into place, but it was too late to halt her progress. The jolt of the frame hitting the first few stairs had her sliding toward the edge of the seat before the careening wheelchair overturned, sending her tumbling headfirst down the stairs. With a sickening crunch, her head collided with one of the steps, compressing her neck and causing the discs to rupture before snapping completely. Instantly numb to any pain, her body continued to tumble, accompanied by a cacophony of dull thuds and sharp cracks. Finally, she came to rest at the foot of the stairs, her head twisted unnaturally.

She blinked in shock, desperately trying to draw in breath, but her twisted airway was completely blocked. The numbness in her limbs did nothing to quell the icy wave of terror that crashed over her as the reality of the situation hit. A harsh crackling, rasping sound reverberated from the broken skin of her neck as the exposed muscles within tried to expand and contract but failed, blood pouring from the ruptured veins within. From her vantage point, she could just make out the hallway and the front door.

"Ready or not, here I come," Tommy's voice was faint, lost in the deafening ringing that filled her head.

Black spots danced in her vision as the small familiar feet of Tommy came speeding into view from the entrance of the lounge room and skidded to an abrupt stop, the cup full of water he had been holding hitting the ground and soaking his socks. Behind him, the front door opened. The last thing she saw was Boyd's legs sprinting toward her before she fell into eternal darkness.

Chapter 17
Boyd

Boyd pulled the Land Rover into the driveway, wincing as he put the car in park and turned the ignition off. Flipping down the mirror, he examined himself, turning his head from side to side. Numerous nicks and cuts criss crossed his face; while most were dried, several fresher wounds bled down his neck, staining his shirt collar.

The cuts on his face paled in comparison to the rest of his body. Both his arms were covered in cuts and bruises, his shirt ripped and torn in spots, exposing further bloody gashes. His legs weren't in much better condition than his arms. He cursed to himself, leaning his forehead onto the sun-kissed warm leather of the wheel.

As an arborist, cuts and scrapes were a part of the trade and something that he had gotten used to very quickly. Despite the inherent risks, he had been lucky to avoid any major injuries from falls or tree branches collapsing from underneath him. That was until today. After two nights of lacklustre sleep and his thoughts occupied with Isla, Tommy, and that... thing... Bobby, his concentration had been compromised. Had he been more alert, he would have noticed the telltale signs of the weak branch he was alighting on and chosen a safer position. Unfortunately, by the time he had recognized the danger, it was too late.

Before he knew it, the branch had snapped off, sending him plummeting to the ground with it. Luckily for him, he had been on a lower branch of the immense oak tree he had been working on, so the fall wasn't as damaging as it could have been. All the same, he was lucky to have escaped with just some cuts and scrapes. Most falls like his would usually have resulted in at least one broken bone, something he and his family could not afford on top of everything else.

The fall had at least given him an excuse to leave work even earlier than expected though, which he was thankful for. At least as banged up as he was, he could give Isla a bit of relief and a chance to rest. He could also call back Janet from whom he had a couple of missed calls and a message asking him to contact her as soon as possible. In the chaos of the accident and its aftermath, calling her back had completely slipped his mind.

With one final deep breath, he exited the car, closing the door and locking it with a beep of his fob. Approaching the front door, he fumbled with his keys, his mind preoccupied with the upcoming call with Janet concerning Bobby. There was no doubt Bobby's removal would cause further damage to Tommy's already fragile mental state, so before he made the call, he needed to talk to Isla to come up with a plan on how to handle the situation. After a few failed attempts, he had the key in the door and unlocked it, pushing the door open to reveal a scene straight out of a nightmare.

Tommy was standing in the hallway, frozen, an empty cup by his feet, adding its last few drops to a puddle surrounding his wet socks. He was staring toward the stairs where the twisted and broken body of Isla lay, her eyes displaying a tiny spark of awareness before it faded away before his eyes. With one last shuddering twitch, her body stilled, as the blood continued to flow from the deep gash in her neck, the exposed bone stark and white against the dark crimson.

"I...Isla? Isla! No, Isla No!"

A desperate cry tore from Boyd's throat as he rushed toward Isla, a blur of motion as he hurtled past Tommy, desperate to see if there was any chance she could be saved, knowing in his heart there wasn't, but refusing to believe it. He stumbled, his knees buckling as he reached her, her lifeless body sprawled before him. An icy wave of numbness washed over him, paralyzing him with shock. He reached toward her neck for a pulse, but the mangled flesh offered no place to feel for one. He reached for her hand, clasping it in his own, feeling the warmth already slipping away from her once vibrant flesh. His mind couldn't process the thought that she was dead, rejecting it with a fierce, instinctual denial. He placed his fingers on her wrist, still searching for a pulse that was not there. The truth finally began to sink into his tortured mind, seeping in like a slow, freezing tide. He felt his chest constrict, a crushing pressure that made it hard to breathe, the sudden lump in his throat making it even harder. Tears formed, stinging his eyes, held back from falling only because of the sheer intensity of his grief as a silent scream began to claw at his throat, desperate for release.

"Daddy? D... Daddy? Is Mommy ok? Mommy will be ok, won't she?" Tommy's hesitant fear filled voice came from just behind him as his small hand came to rest on his shoulder.

In an instant, Boyd's paternal instinct kicked in, an urge to protect his son from the traumatic scene in front of him prompting him to turn away from Isla. He buried Tommy in an embrace, shielding him from the horrific sight. He rocked him in his arms, the comforting words he longed to speak stuck in his throat, unable to bypass the lump there. His devastation threatened to give way to a torrent of tears and grief. Tommy's body began to tremble against his, shock beginning to take hold of his small, fragile body before it gave way to heaving sobs. Boyd clasped Tommy's head to his chest, tears spilling from his own eyes. He struggled to contain the overwhelming emotions threatening to render him helpless and unable to provide the comfort Tommy so desperately needed.

A low feral growl from behind him, heavy with menace, stopped his rocking. Boyd stiffened, every hair on his neck prickling with dread. The growl was full of primal rage and hunger and spoke of barely contained animalistic ferocity. Conscious of every movement, Boyd released his grip on Tommy. Tommy looked at him in alarm, his small arms extending toward him, trying to cuddle him once more, but Boyd held him at arm's length, his eyes softening with a mixture of love and sorrow, yearning to give Tommy what he needed but knowing he couldn't.

"Tommy, when I tell you, I need you to run to the kitchen and use the telephone to call the police, ok? The number is 911."

Tommy just stood there staring at him, a mixture of confusion, fear, hurt, and pain on his tear-streaked face.

Behind Boyd, the growling grew louder and more insistent. Boyd knew that they only had a matter of seconds before the creature behind him launched its attack.

"Tommy, did you hear me? I need you to be brave for me, just one more time, ok? Can you do it for me? Can you make the call?"

Tommy nodded fearfully, his eyes widening as they caught movement behind Boyd, giving Boyd enough warning to get his next words out.

"Now! go!"

He spun around, his arms covering his head, just as Bobby's small, hard form crashed into his chest. A searing pain shot through Boyd as Bobby's extended claws ripped and tore through his shirt to the skin beneath. Blood sprayed from his eviscerated flesh, coating the walls of the hallway as he stumbled backwards, his arms clawing at the ferocious bundle of fur and muscle who had already torn a ragged gash deep through his chest into the tendons and muscles beneath.

Managing to pry the relentless creature away, he hurled it towards the nearest wall with all his might. The creature shrieked as it struck the wall, a bone-jarring thud echoing through the room before it fell to the ground, silent. Its large, bulbous eyes, still open and burning with hate, were fixed on him, but it lay frozen on the floor, its body quivering as if from shock.

Using the opportunity, Boyd stumbled backwards down the hall toward the kitchen, keeping his eye on the creature. Behind him, he could hear Tommy on the phone, screaming for help.

Blood seeped out from his wound in a relentless tide, soaking the torn fabric of his shirt and spilling to the floor. He gritted his teeth, his breath rasping as he pressed his hand firmly against it, searching desperately for something to stem the flow. Spotting a washcloth on the back of a kitchen chair, he turned toward it, only to collapse to the floor as Bobby's powerful, directed strikes tore and sliced through his calf muscles from behind. His chest hit the floor with a sickening wet squelch, blood spraying in all directions from the impact. His vision swam as he kicked, desperately trying to dislodge Bobby, who had buried his teeth into the gaping calf wound, the sound of ripping and tearing flesh filling the kitchen. Behind him, Tommy's shrill screams of terror echoed through the air as he dropped the phone with a thud and scrambled backwards on the floor against the kitchen cabinet.

Boyd raised his other foot, screaming in pain, and brought it down with force onto Bobby's head. His strike was weak, but it was enough to temporarily stun the creature, who tumbled to the floor, a sizable chunk of Boyd's bloody calf muscle still in his mouth. Taking advantage of the reprieve, Boyd crawled toward the base of the kitchen counter, leaving bloody trails behind him, feeling himself grow weaker with each agonizing movement.

He glanced toward Tommy, who had retreated into the corner of the kitchen and curled himself into a tight ball. He was rocking back and forth, his body wracked with sobs. Seeing his son so vulnerable, so torn apart by the trauma he had seen and already been through, gave him the boost of strength to go on. He needed to protect Tommy; he had failed at doing that all year. He would fight for him to his very last dying breath.

He had reached the base of the kitchen counter when he heard the creature stirring behind him. He was running out of time.

With a strangled cry of pain, he reached up and gripped the edge of the counter with both hands, using his upper body to pull himself upwards, all sensation in his legs now lost. His head rose above the counter and swivelled toward the knife rack in front of him. Extending his arm toward it, his fingertips grazed the base of it, but there wasn't enough leverage to grasp it completely.

Behind him, he could hear Bobby growling in rage and the rapidly approaching clicking of claws on the kitchen floor tiles. With one last effort, he pulled himself up further, letting out another scream of pain as his chest wound scraped against the corner of the counter. Using the last of his strength, he grasped the knife rack and dragged it toward him, releasing it to grab the nearest knife and wrench it free.

A searing, sharp tear in his lower back sent a shockwave of excruciating pain through his body, making Boyd cry out as he threw himself backward, hoping to crush Bobby beneath him. He crashed to the floor, his ruined body landing with a sickening wet slap onto the blood-soaked tiles, as Bobby leaped aside at the last moment, narrowly avoiding the impact. Picking himself up, Bobby approached him slowly, a cruel, sadistic smile transforming into a snarl, his quivering lips retracting to reveal his sharp, bloodstained teeth. Thick crimson drool dripped from the edges of his mouth as the creature studied him with undisguised hunger.

Gasping for air, Boyd lay there, his lungs filling with blood, the sickening sounds of rattling and popping echoing with each strained breath. A whirlwind of memories and regrets flashed before him, each one hitting him with a sharp pang of what once was and would never be again. He fought to stay awake as pain surged through his body, each wave more intense than the last, yet he clung to consciousness with a ferocious determination. Tommy's bright eyes and loving smile filled his thoughts. It was a vivid image that gave him the strength he needed to endure, to hold on just a little longer. Every breath- every heartbeat he had left, was a reminder of the life he had to protect and fight for.

As his heartbeat faltered, he forced himself to whisper Tommy's name. As the world around him blurred and faded, the thought of his son remained clear, a beacon of hope among the growing darkness. He could not afford to let go now, not yet. He tightened his grip on the knife by his side, hidden from view by the approaching Bobby, praying for a chance to use it before he faded away completely.

Just as he was about to give up hope, Bobby crawled up onto his chest and sat there, cocking his head to the side in curiosity as he watched Boyd's life fade away before his eyes. So mesmerized was he by the sight that he failed to notice the knife swinging down from above until it was too late to avoid.

The knife struck with all the force that Boyd had left, slipping with ease into the top of Bobby's head. It punched through his skull into the flesh of his brain and down through his throat and stomach before exiting, only to plunge down into Boyd's chest, then through into his own heart. The pair lay there motionless, pinned together by the knife, both bodies torn and bloodied.

Boyd's final thought was a prayer for Tommy, a hope that he would carry on, that he would someday, somehow, recover from the tragedies and trauma he had suffered before Boyd knew no more. His arm fell to the floor lifeless as blood continued to spill from both his and Bobby's ruined bodies. The only sounds left in the house were Tommy's moans, sobs, and sniffles, a symphony of his grief as he continued to rock back and forth in the corner opposite the bloody, lifeless bodies of his father and his rogue pet.

Chapter 18

Tommy

Tommy rocked back and forth, his body desperate for solace, for some semblance of comfort from the chaos in his mind even as it began to retreat into itself, building walls between him and reality to protect him from the unbearable trauma. The floor melted away beneath him just as the room around him did, blurring and fading into a distant haze, every detail, every feeling melting away into obscurity.

Memories rose unbidden to his mind in a last-ditch effort to penetrate the barriers he had built, but they slipped through like sand as his subconscious mind sought to protect him from the immensity of the pain he would otherwise have felt.

As his father took his last breath, Tommy found himself in a place of solace. A sanctuary of his own creation deep within his mind, untouched by fear, pain and anguish. Here, there was only happiness, the sun always shone, and flowers were perpetually in bloom, offering their sweet scent to those lucky enough to pass by.

The world felt like a vibrant playground; though their faces were strangely absent, every person who lived here oozed joy, its infectious, comforting presence seeping into his body. Here, the raging beast of trauma that existed just beyond the border could not penetrate. Here he was safe, cocooned in the gentle embrace of comfort and forgetfulness.

Tommy kept rocking, a wide smile on his face through his drying tears as he stared into the distance unseeingly, lost within himself as the world outside dripped with blood.

Chapter 19

Jonathan

Jonathan sighed, gripping the wheel of his van, preparing himself for the inevitable tirade of anger he would receive when he knocked on the O'Halloran's door.

He had arrived hopeful that he could speak directly to Isla, but his stomach had sunk when he saw the familiar Land Rover belonging to Boyd parked in the driveway. He must have taken the day off to look after Isla.

Being a journalist had its perks, but it also had some major drawbacks. Dealing with angry people was one of them, but it was part of the job. He had learned very quickly to develop a thick skin and not take things personally, but there was always an element of anxiety leading up to such a confrontation. He could only hope that Boyd had calmed down enough that he could get a few words at least, perhaps even sneak in a photo of this mysterious creature. Tucking his notepad and pen into his breast pocket, he emerged from his van, taking the opportunity to stretch. His back was starting to play up a bit lately, a victim of his constant hunching, a bad habit he had developed when writing in his notebook or laptop, often in haste.

Taking a few more calming breaths, he walked toward the O'Halloran's house, the quiet of the neighbourhood broken only by the distant chirp of birds. It was as perfect a day as one could expect on Halloween. The sun was at its zenith, with not a cloud in sight. The trees were shedding their few remaining leaves, which twirled and danced in the cool breeze before settling on the ground, joining their fallen brethren. The air was crisp and fresh, ready to welcome the rush of happy children that would flow down the streets later in the afternoon.

As he walked down the path approaching the front door, he could see that it was ajar, the door swaying slightly with each gust of the gentle wind. Leaves had started to make their way inside through the gap into the hallway beyond.

Jonathan frowned, instantly on guard. He crept onto the porch, ears straining for any noise inside. At first, he heard nothing, but as he neared the open door, he could hear the muted sound of the TV coming from further within. On the verge of knocking, he hesitated. A rhythmic tapping, a softer sound nearby, was almost imperceptible above the sound of the TV.

He knocked on the doorframe loudly.

"Hello? Mr O'Halloran?"

There was no answer. The sound of the TV and the rhythmic tapping continued as he debated going inside.

"Hello? Anyone home?"

He hesitated for a few moments, feeling a prickle of unease, before finally deciding to enter. If either Mr or Mrs O'Halloran were inside and saw him, he could always use the open door as an excuse, but he had a horrible feeling he wouldn't need to.

He stepped inside cautiously. The inside of the house was dark, a stark contrast to the bright sunshine outside. He waited a moment and strained to hear any further sounds as he waited for his eyes to adjust to the sudden change in light. Muffled sounds of a news report about a scientific experiment gone wrong drifted from the lounge room TV, the images from the screen casting shadows on the floor tiles before him.

Ignoring it, he took a few more steps forward, pausing as his eyes widened, pupils dilating in disbelief at the shocking sight before him. Isla's broken body lay at the foot of the stairs, a grotesque tableau of twisted limbs and exposed, blood-soaked neck bones. Crimson blood pooled on the hallway tiles, spreading like a dark stain.

He was jolted out of his shock by his phone buzzing in his pocket. He fished for it absently, his gaze still fixed on the horrific scene before him, breaking it long enough to glance down at the message. It was from Emily, his wife, reminding him to pick up their son from school, as she was stuck in meetings all day.

He dropped the phone back into his pocket, the rhythmic tapping from further on in the house capturing his attention as it continued. It sounded like it was coming from the kitchen just around the bend in the hallway.

He approached hesitantly, his dread intensifying with every step. He reached the kitchen doorway and halted, a sickly pallor overtaking his features. Directly ahead of him was the ravaged body of Boyd with the mangled creature pinned to him with the large kitchen knife. He averted his gaze and emptied his stomach onto the floor, the smell of bile mixing with the other bodily fluids already covering the sticky surface.

The persistent tapping continued, capturing his attention as he wiped his mouth, the acrid bile still coating his tongue. The tapping came from the corner where Tommy sat, rocking back and forth on the floor, his scuffed sneakers slapping against the kitchen tiles. His movements were slow and rhythmic, his wide eyes staring blankly ahead, unseeing and distant.

The haunting emptiness in his eyes contrasted sharply with the joyful smile plastered on his face, as if he were lost in a world of his own, oblivious to the horrific surroundings. His hands were wrapped around his knees, knuckles white from his tight grip as he continued to rock back and forth, back and forth. It was as if he was trapped in a loop, unable or unwilling to break free from the invisible chains that bound him.

Sorrow filled Jonathan at the sight. Seeing the small vulnerable boy in front of him, clearly traumatized to the point where he had withdrawn completely from the world, broke his heart. Tears rose unbidden in his eyes. The desire to comfort the boy was strong, but he knew there was nothing he could do. He was beyond the help that Jonathan could offer, perhaps beyond anyone's help.

The distant sound of wailing sirens approaching tore his gaze away toward the front door. It was time to let the professionals handle this. Despite the horrific and heartbreaking scene, he had to write the story and get comments from the paramedics and police on their conclusions. As he made his way to the front door, the news story playing in the lounge room made him pause.

"... NeuroBalance Institute, a biotech company. According to sources, the experiment had been rushed through approval without sufficient testing. The results speak for themselves. Out of the twenty families these creatures have gone to, there have been fourteen fatalities reported in the last twenty-four hours. NeuroBalance Institute representatives had been sent to the first sites in an attempt to salvage and cover up the fatalities, but several ended up fatalities themselves. One such fatality, the head of customer service, Janet Palmer was found with her throat torn out at the Peterson household, one of the first to receive a Bliss Buddy. The entire family had been slaughtered by the creature, the creature itself reportedly missing from the scene leading to grave fears it may be loose..."

With a frown of concern, Jonathan jotted down a note to follow up on the missing Bliss Buddy. He shook his head sadly, recalling the small creature pinned to Boyd's chest. Walking outside the front door, he stepped to the side and leaned his head back against the brick wall as the flashing blue and red lights of the first police car skidded to a halt in the street in front of him. His thoughts turned to Tommy, the small broken boy who was perhaps beyond help. Maybe, against all odds, he could. Michael, his son, was similar in age and had always asked for a brother. From the limited research he was able to do, he knew the boy didn't have any relatives left. He would have to see what eventuated from this tragedy first. If there was any opportunity to take him in, he would do it. He needed to run it past Emily first. He was confident she wouldn't need much persuading; after all, they had been trying for another child for years, and lately, they'd been discussing the possibility of adoption.

Sometimes, in the face of overwhelming darkness, all you can do is extend a hand, be that tiny flicker of light that pierces the gloom. Jonathan would be that light if given the chance. A guide to lead Tommy through the shadows and into a brighter future no matter how long the journey would be and where it would take them.